W9-DHG-091

Giraffe of Montana

VOLUME III

William Bowman Piper

Little Pemberley Press
Houston, TX
2007

Little Pemberley Press
1528 Tulane Street, Suite F
Houston, TX 77008
713-862-8542

www.GiraffeofMontana.com

ISBN# 978-09763359-6-2

Piper, William Bowman, 1927-
Giraffe of Montana / by William Bowman Piper.
p. cm. — (Giraffe of Montana ; v. 3)
SUMMARY: A giraffe living in Montana and his animal friends share adventures and the ups and downs of daily life.
Audience: Ages 6-12.
ISBN 978-0-9763359-6-2
1. Animals—Juvenile fiction. [1. Animals—Fiction.
2. Friendship—Fiction. 3. Montana—Fiction.] I. Title.

PZ10.3.P412Gir 2007 [E] QBI05-600033

Book Production Team
Consulting & Coordination — Rita Mills of The Book Connection
Editing — Faye Walker

Cover Design & Illustrations — Bill Megenhardt

The paper used in this publication meets the requirements of the American National Standard for Permanence of Paper for Printed Library Materials Z39.48-1984.

Printed in the United States of America

to my grandchildren,

Benjamin,
Allison,
Elias, and
Cosmo

Acknowledgements

The author wishes once again to thank
Rita Mills, the compositor and publishing consultant,
Bill Megenhardt, the illustrator and cover designer,
and Faye Walker, the editor.

Stories

An Errand of Mercy

✠ ✠ ✠

Giraffe was galloping in the meadow near his cave one bright October day in the company of Zane and Zack the zebras. He needed, as he explained, to exercise his legs. According to Dr. Oscar the orangutan, he told them, his left hind leg especially had become very arthritic.

"'If you don't exercise,' the doctor warned me, 'I may have to replace your hip, and that is a very serious operation for a giraffe.'"

Oddly, this made Zane and Zack break out laughing.

Giraffe had just come from visiting the palace; and the king's frailty, which made Giraffe cut his visit short, plus his own decrepitude had undermined his usual good cheer. Such painful exercise didn't help. Nevertheless, there he was galloping for his health although, as he complained a little to his unsympathetic companions, the effort made his old bones ache.

"Buck up, Giraffe," Zack advised him. "Princess Isabel has begun taking on the responsibilities of royalty—and found herself a well-educated assistant. No matter what happens to you now, the future is secure for all us Montanans."

"I suppose you are right, Zack," Giraffe admitted.

But this assurance, he realized to his surprise, did not make him feel much better.

"Of course, it is comforting," he said as he limped and loped along, "to know the princess is finding herself at last and to know Montana will be in good hands when the king and I are no longer around."

His striped friends, he noticed with a twinge of envy, raced across the meadow as easily as ever, so he stretched out his legs, neglected the pain, and tried to keep up.

The three of them reached the edge of the woods where Giraffe made a rather awkward spin. His cell phone rang.

Isabel, who had married King Arthur a few years before and joined him at Camelot in the southeast corner of the state, had given it to Giraffe last Christmas at the celebration in Friendship Hall. "So," as she explained, "we can remain in touch. I didn't realize before I married and moved away how big Montana is."

The phone, which hung by a little chain around Giraffe's neck, had been especially designed for his use. He could lift it with his tongue, attach it with little hooks to his horns and then both hear and speak quite at his ease.

"Giraffe," said Queen Isabel, "is that you?"

"As if it could have been anyone else," he thought before answering.

"Yes, your majesty," he said once he gained his breath. "Giraffe here. Are you okay?"

"Yes, Giraffe, the king and I are fine."

"I'm glad," he wheezed. "I thought I heard anxiety in your voice."

"No," the queen assured him. "We're fine. But we do have a problem, Giraffe: a loose dragon."

"A loose dragon? I thought you and King Arthur had established peace with the dragon community."

"We did, Giraffe, and we live in harmony with them—most of them. Several dragons work here in the castle—to cook, to serve, to escort guests. The roasts provided by Persimmon, whose hot breath is a legend, are delicious. But one of them, Persimmon's son Charlton, in fact, has recently gone wild and turned on us."

"Charlton, Mango's big brother?"

"Yes, Giraffe, Charlton. He has become transformed into what Sir Lancelot has described as 'the cheese fiend'—that silly Lancelot—and he afflicts us all the time."

"I remember him, your majesty, although, as you know, I am more closely acquainted with his little sister, who visited us here in the middle of Montana last spring. He was a big oafish fellow, a bit of an embarrassment to his family, but quite harmless."

"That's the one, but he's grown, he's developed a terribly fiery breath, greater than his father's, and, for some reason, he's decided to aim it at Camelot. Will you come and help us, Giraffe? We live in fear and trembling, the king and I and all the knights of the Round Table."

"Sir Lancelot and Sir Gawain, trembling with fear?"

"Yes, Giraffe, they're just as scared as the rest. So you can see why Arthur and I need your help."

"I'll take the train today, your majesty, if Billy the beaver can attach my car. Is there a little more you can tell me right now?"

"No, Giraffe, we'll tell you the whole story, King Arthur and I, as soon as you arrive. Please hurry."

"Of course, your majesty," he replied. "I'd fly over with Roo if I could."

Queen Isabel's call for help made Giraffe very happy. With the recent maturity of Princess Isabel and her growing reliance on Fergus, which even Zane and Zack had noticed, he had begun to feel his usefulness in Montana was coming to an end.

"But not yet," he said to himself as he made arrangements with Billy the beaver for his journey to Camelot. "Not yet."

The Camelot train station, which had been built as a chapel in the olden days, had a beautiful stone steeple at one end, a pair of stone towers at the other, and a sign over the door that opened into the waiting room, which read, "King Arthur and his knights of the Round Table welcome you to Camelot." Queen Isabel waited as the Montana train drew in; then she raced down the platform to Giraffe's car so she could greet him as soon as Billy the beaver lowered the gangplank and let him descend.

"Oh, Giraffe," she cried as he reached the platform. "I'm so glad to see you. We need your help. The king and I are at our wits' end—and his knights, his knights are no use at all."

"The knights? Sir Lancelot? Sir Gawain? Young Galahad with his sparkling new armor? No use at all?"

"None, Giraffe, and Charlton has killed a couple of our lesser knights. That's why I had to call you."

She continued after they had started off together for the castle. "He swoops into the hall, scorching our tapestries with his disgusting breath and landing right in the middle of the Round Table. The knights raise such a clatter getting away from him that the king can't call anyone else to help us—not that there is anyone."

"Disgusting?" Giraffe exclaimed in surprise. "Is Charlton's fiery breath disgusting?"

"Yes, Giraffe, disgusting. It smells like rotten fruit, rotten bananas, really. But the king and I will tell you everything once we get to the castle."

"Rotten bananas," Giraffe murmured thoughtfully as he and the queen walked along. "Rotten bananas? Very interesting."

"Interesting?" the queen responded. "Maybe, but really nauseating. You don't like bananas, Giraffe. You never ate those Gloria the gorilla kept hanging up in your cave, and you never tried her famous banana punch, did you?"

"No," Giraffe replied with a smile. "I dislike bananas in all forms. Nevertheless, Charlton's hot banana breath I find very interesting."

✠ ✠ ✠

The main castle of Camelot, which rose on an old Viking mound about half of a mile from the station, was designed by a couple of architects who had stopped by to consult with King Arthur a few years before on their way from Hollywood to Orlando. It featured a massive, imitation-granite curtain, to which an array of durable plastic turrets and, actually, of turrets upon turrets with steep, sparkling roofs were attached.

"It's a little drafty," Queen Isabel confessed to Giraffe as they crossed the moat on an elegant plastic drawbridge and approached what exactly resembled a steel portcullis. "It's not cozy like Daddy's palace in the middle of Montana, but it gives the right impression.

"My heroic mate insists no castle is complete," she explained as they waited for admittance, "without a retractable portcullis. A man's castle," she said with a smile, "is his castle."

Once inside, Giraffe and the queen were ushered by two comely young dragons, Peach and Nectarine, into the royal banquet hall, a round room with the Round Table at its center. Across from the door, on a chair slightly raised above all the others placed around the table, sat King Arthur.

He was somewhat older than his queen, to be sure, but he was hearty. His hair was growing gray, and he looked a little weather-beaten.

"Twelve major battles," as Giraffe reminded himself, "will have that effect."

But the king was a fine, big man with majestic bearing, and he wore his gold-plated crown at a jaunty angle. He was, moreover, devoted to his young queen, on whom, as she and Giraffe entered the hall, he looked with obvious pride and affection.

"Ah, Giraffe," he said as Isabel embraced him. "You see before you a happy couple. Does it surprise you?"

"I sometimes wonder, your majesty," he answered, "how you and Isabel discovered one another although your conjugal happiness is evident."

"Her father and I, Giraffe," said the king, "often talked together over our mead, reliving the old days when we fought the Saxons and others to protect the Borders. And my darling girl, who replenished our mugs, drank in my tales of peril and victory as avidly as her father and I drank in our mead. She always asked me to repeat the stories she had missed while she was attending to our needs.

"Soon I recognized, and I returned, the growing warmth she showed. She loved me for the dangers I had passed, Giraffe, and I loved her because she pitied them."

"I understand, your majesty, and I congratulate you both on your marriage and your happiness."

"Thank you, Giraffe," said the queen somewhat impatiently as she brushed an erring lock of hair back under her husband's crown. "But aren't we forgetting, my dear, the reason for Giraffe's visit to Camelot?"

"True, my love," said the king. "Thank you for reminding us."

And he smiled up at her with a lively twinkle in his eye.

"She could have done worse," Giraffe thought to himself. "Fergus and Isabel in the middle of Montana, if it comes to that; Arthur and Isabel here. I will be leaving the state in very good hands."

"Giraffe," said the king after he had kissed his Isabel, "as the queen reminds us both, she and I have a serious need for your counsel."

"I will be happy," Giraffe replied with as low a bow as his old joints would permit, "to serve you, in any way I can."

"The queen has no doubt sketched our problem," Arthur said as he settled his crown more firmly. "But perhaps I can fill in the details."

"I would like to know as much as you are able to tell me," Giraffe responded. "The more I know, the more I can help. I'm especially interested, as I told the queen while we waited for the portcullis to be lifted, in Charlton's banana breath."

"All in good time, Giraffe. But first let me explain how this renegade invades us. He furls his wings and dives through one of those big windows; then stretching his wings, he circles the room, breathing the noxious fire the queen has obviously described to you, and lights on the Round Table, isn't that right, Isabel my love?"

"Yes, Arthur my dear; and he's been plaguing us, Giraffe, for more than three months now, crashing down among the plates and bowls and tumblers—always during the supper hour—two or three times a week.

"Just look at the scratches those great claws of his have made on our table," the queen complained. "They'll never come out."

"The table seems to be made of real wood, your majesty," said Giraffe, examining it closely.

"It is, Giraffe," she replied with satisfaction. "Solid mahogany." And she flicked it a couple of times with her fingernail.

"On his first appearance," the king continued, "he killed two of my knights, Agravayne and Palomides. He roasted them, Giraffe," the king recalled, shaking his head in dismay. "You're famous, as my dear wife has reminded me, for solving Montana's problems, but this one may prove to be too tough even for you."

"Perhaps, your majesty, but I am ready to try." After a pause, he asked, "Has Charlton killed anyone since that first appearance?"

"No," the king replied. "Only that first time."

"Tell me about it, your majesty, tell me about that first time."

"Would you like to tell Giraffe about it, Isabel? You probably remember it more clearly than I do."

"No, my dear; you begin and I'll add anything you leave out."

"We were feasting one night last summer," the king began. "It was June, and my dear love and I were celebrating our wedding anniversary. It was a wonderful occasion. You know, Giraffe, I loved my first wife, Guinevere, and her conduct, especially her eloping with young Mordred, made me very unhappy for a while. But it left me free to choose again, and to choose better. Marrying Isabel, have I told you, Giraffe, is the best thing I ever did."

"Yes, my dear," said Isabel, interrupting her lord. "It has been fortunate for me, too. But aren't you losing the thread?"

"True, my dear," said the king with a smile.

"Well, we had finished our meat and got on to the fruit and cheese and nuts. I especially like bananas, Giraffe, and the young dragons who escorted you through the palace peel them for me along with peaches and nectarines, of course, and serve them around the table in a great bronze bowl. We get them from your friend, Gloria the gorilla, who mails a stalk to us—"

"Your majesty," Queen Isabel interposed somewhat severely, "aren't you losing the thread again?"

"Yes, my dear," the king admitted. "Thank you for recalling me.

"Before we could help ourselves to this delectable course, a great blast of heat enveloped the room. 'Is it the Grail?' exclaimed Lancelot, who has always been obsessed with that old myth."

"That Lancelot," muttered the queen.

"But it wasn't. It was a great dragon whose wings, when he extended them, almost filled the hall. It was Charlton, as we later identified him. He swooped through the window, circled the company, and, while still blowing a terrible flame, perched on the Round Table. Then he began gobbling our cheese and bananas. A funny thing, Giraffe—he didn't touch the nuts, and we had a pretty silver dish full of very tasty ones, cashews, walnuts, almonds, macadamias. I especially relish the macadamias, Giraffe, which Billy the beaver transports over here after they have been flown to Billings all the way from Hawaii."

"My dear," said Queen Isabel.

"Yes, yes, I'm losing the thread again. Well, to continue, the first one of us to recover from the shock of Charlton's entrance was Gawain's pesky little brother, Agravayne, isn't that right, Isabel?"

"True," said the queen. "It was Agravayne."

"He was affronted," said the king, "that a dragon, uninvited, should enter the royal hall."

"That was Agravayne," said the queen. "Open-mouthed as always."

"'What right have you,' he shouted at the intruder while waving his sword about, 'to crash our banquet and take a seat at the Round Table?'"

"That was Agravayne," said the queen.

"Actually, Giraffe," the king said with a little laugh, "Charlton was taking a seat *on* the Round Table, as my queen has explained.

"When he heard Agravayne shouting and saw him brandish his sword," the king continued, "he turned his head and exhaled, and that was the end of Agravayne. He was roasted in red-hot armor, Giraffe, roasted to a turn. Charlton, by the way, is the son of our chief cook, Persimmon—and a very good cook too, isn't he my love? His pork chops, his pastry, his filet mignon—"

"Excuse me, your majesty," Giraffe interrupted before the queen could interrupt. "Did Charlton's breath smell of bananas on this occasion?"

"I don't think so. Did it, my dear?"

"No," said the queen, "not that first time, but it has every time since, and what an offensive smell."

"I believe, my love," Arthur said, "that Giraffe has a notion about that smell, haven't you, Giraffe?"

"A suspicion, your majesty; but I'd like you to finish your account of that night, if you would."

"Surely, Giraffe," the king agreed. "When Charlton turned toward Agravayne, I believe Palomides thought he was about to threaten the queen—a gallant knight, Palomides, even if he is—was—a saracen. At any rate, he drew his weapon and thrust it into Charlton's side; it was a real thrust, Giraffe, a real wound. When the dragon felt it, he aimed his breath at Palomides and roasted him, too.

"Then he turned his scaly head this way and that, surveying our food; and when he located what he wanted, the cheese and the bananas, as I told you, Giraffe, he devoured them, leaving the nuts and most of the other fruit untouched. After he had finished, he gave his great wings a twitch that almost extinguished our lamps and departed the same way he had come."

"What about Lancelot and the other knights?" asked Giraffe. "What did they do all this time?"

"Lancelot and the others?" cried the queen. "They scurried toward the wall as fast as their bow legs would carry them, regretting, I'm sure, that the hall didn't have any corners for them to hide in."

"The dragon's appearance was so sudden, Giraffe, and so unexpected," the king insisted, "bursting here into the heart of the castle. He was enormous, besides. He seemed to fill the hall. His eyes rolled and sparkled, his snout was horribly wrinkled, and his great flaming mouth was always agape. Each of his teeth, Giraffe, seemed almost a foot long, and he roared like a blast furnace as he descended on us. Anyone would have quailed at that moment. I can't complain of my knights."

"I can," cried Queen Isabel. "I expected better of Lancelot—the mighty Lancelot—and Galahad and the whole circle. The king remained steady on his throne, Giraffe, and, in my concern for him, I stayed by his side. But his famous knights, except for the brat and the saracen, were saturated with fright."

"That's not quite fair, my love. If Lancelot and the others have time to consider, they are very brave men. In all the dragon's attacks since the first, they have held their seats and refrained from attacking him only at my command. They are ready to a knight, Giraffe, to act if I should order action or, if the queen should be in danger, to protect her. However, I have decided Charlton must be allowed his bananas and his cheese unhindered, and, because of this, no one has suffered. Of course, the hall has been singed and blackened, as you can see, Giraffe; the Round Table is scarred; and the odor of rotten fruit hangs over everything. But if I had commanded my knights to fight, Camelot would have been polluted with blood; and even if the monster had been killed, the survivors could not have remained. Now if we can defeat or disperse this scourge, we can resume our lives."

"I agree, your majesty," said Giraffe. "We must remove the scourge from Camelot. And I believe I know how to do that."

"You do?" Queen Isabel exclaimed in disbelief. "Oh, if you save us, Giraffe, we will be eternally grateful, won't we, my king?"

"Yes, my love. We will never forget you, Giraffe, if you free our castle and restore our land."

"I think I can, your majesty. But, first, I must meet with Mango and Persimmon and the whole family of the unfortunate Charlton."

"The unfortunate Charlton?" said King Arthur. "You call the monster unfortunate?"

"Yes, your majesty, unfortunate. You have explained fully he killed only those who attacked him and only in self-defense. He never threatened the queen, I believe, despite what Palomides feared. And since you have restrained your thanes, he has gobbled his bananas and cheese and gone on his way."

"You may be right, Giraffe," said the king thoughtfully. "But we cannot tolerate his coming in on us night after night, devouring our victuals, and trashing our castle."

"No doubt," replied Giraffe, "we must stop him, if we can. And to accomplish that I must meet with his family. After I have had a chance to talk with them, I may need to test the valor of your knights and give at least one of them an opportunity, Queen Isabel, to redeem the Round Table. I especially wish to confront Mango."

"Mango?" said the queen in disbelief. "Little Mango?"

"My dear," said the king, "I see our friend Giraffe has something in mind, although I cannot guess what it is. But a meeting with Mango and her whole family—except for Charlton, of course, whose whereabouts nobody knows—is easily arranged."

✠ ✠ ✠

"He was always a nice kid, Giraffe," said Pineapple and expelled a smoky sigh. "He was, wasn't he, my love?"

"He's clumsy," Persimmon replied with some heat. "He's clumsy. You remember the time, Pine, he knocked over our best lamp with his tail and, in a reflex action, almost got your best vase as well?"

"It was an accident; besides, he cleaned it up, every sliver of it, himself. Charlton has always been very sweet, Giraffe, especially to his little sister."

"Is that true, Mango?" Giraffe asked.

He could hardly see the tiny dragon who lurked in a halo of smoke at the back of the cave.

"Yes, Giraffe," she murmured, turning her eyes away from him. "Charlton is a very good brother."

"Whenever he soared off into the forest—and Charlton has become a very strong flier, as the king no doubt told you—he would take Mango on his back, wouldn't he, darling; and away they would fly. Not only that," his proud mother added, "but he often brought home food: rabbit, pheasant, squirrel, and once a fine turkey, all of them roasted hot and ready to eat. He was especially good at bringing back our supper when he knew Persimmon was cooking up at the castle. I used to hope, although it's hard to believe now, that someday he might succeed his dad as the king's chief cook."

"Well, then, what happened, Persimmon?" Giraffe asked, turning to the monster's father.

"Maybe you should ask his doting mother or his warm-hearted sister," Persimmon responded heatedly. "They're so fond of him."

"Very well. Pineapple," Giraffe asked with a cough, "what happened?"

"It's true, Giraffe, something did happen a few weeks before our son ran away."

"He ran away? Do you know where he went? Pineapple? Mango?"

"No, Giraffe," answered Pineapple. "He just disappeared. He had been acting strangely, wheezing and sputtering and puffing about for several days."

"He did have trouble keeping his cool," Persimmon agreed. "He would blow up at the least thing."

"You thought it was because of Cauliflower Vegetable, didn't you, Mom?"

"Yes, I did. She's Cucumber and Parsnip's daughter, Giraffe. They're farm folk and not really our type."

"Not our type, Pine, my dear!" Persimmon exploded. "They raise the fine fresh produce I roast for the king. My wife, Giraffe, believes, because I work at the castle, we are too good for the Vegetables."

"That's not it, Giraffe," Pineapple fumed. "But their daughter, Cauliflower, is such a flirt. I see her all the time polishing her scales with bark, scouring her teeth in the sand, and coloring her claws with blackberry juice; then she admires herself in the stream. And what a snout she has! I just thought our Charlton could do a lot better for himself—once the time came."

"But that wasn't the problem, Mom, was it?" Mango burst out.

"No," Pineapple admitted with a sigh; she dropped a couple of scalding tears. "When I mentioned Cauliflower, he just puffed and smoked. No, it wasn't Cauliflower, for all her primping."

"What was it then?" Giraffe asked.

"I don't know, Giraffe, and neither does Persimmon although he and I have had several hot discussions about it. We just don't know."

"But Mango knows," said Giraffe, bending again toward Charlton's little sister. "Isn't that so, Mango?"

"Yes," Mango whispered. "But I can't tell you, Giraffe. I promised."

"But that was before Charlton began to attack the castle, wasn't it? That was when he first told you."

"Told her what?" Persimmon flared out. "Told you what, Mango?"

"Go on, Mango," said Giraffe, coughing partially in sympathy as the smoke settled. "You can tell us now. You must if you want us to help him."

"It's his tooth, Giraffe, his wisdom tooth. The gum that surrounds it is so swollen and infected," Mango sighed through a little ring of smoke, "Charlton can't even close his mouth; he can't clamp his teeth shut."

"I see," Giraffe responded. "He can still roast food, but he can't eat it; he can't even carry it back to his family."

"That's right. He was very embarrassed not to be able to use his teeth; and that molar hurt, Giraffe, it hurt real bad. One time he used his claws to bring food home—it was that pheasant, Mom, do you remember?—and he tore it all to pieces."

"Yes," said Giraffe, "a dragon who can't close his mouth faces a very embarrassing problem—and a very perilous one."

"I remember now," said his mother, kindling on the edge of tears. "He used his breath to heat up some turkey broth I made him one night, and he did take a little of that."

"It was all you could do, Mom, but it wasn't enough," said Mango. "Then one night, Dad brought home some stories about the raw fruit and the cheese that were served at the castle. He went on about the great bowl of peeled bananas and the soft cheeses, the Liederkrantz, the Brie, the Camembert, the Port du Salut."

"Ah," murmured Giraffe to himself, "bananas and Liederkrantz.

"And that night," he said aloud, "Charlton left home, isn't that true, Mango?"

"Yes, Giraffe," she sighed.

After a pause, he bent down and spoke in a very serious tone of voice. "Where did he go?"

"I don't think I know, Giraffe," Mango sobbed through a little puff. "I don't really know."

"If you want to help him, Mango, you must take me to him."

✠ ✠ ✠

"I need a knight," Giraffe announced, addressing the assembled Round Table, "a knight of great strength and courage, a very small knight."

"What you need, Giraffe," said young Galahad, leaping up from his place next to King Arthur, "is a big knight, a big man for a big dragon. And I'm the biggest knight at the Round Table, even bigger than my dad. Show me this monster, and I'll ride against him."

"No, Sir Galahad," Giraffe responded. "Although I have the greatest respect for your strength and courage, your shoulders, especially encased in your fine, clanking armor, are much too big and much too noisy for the quest that confronts the Round Table at this time."

"Too big and too noisy?" the queen echoed with wonder.

"Yes, my lady," Giraffe answered.

"You are famous for solving problems in the middle of Montana, Giraffe," cried Sir Lancelot, who sat next to his son, "but I'm afraid this case of ours is a little beyond you. It will actually require two knights or maybe three. Gawain and I mounted with lances on either side of Charlton, while Galahad keeps him busy in front, will fix a sting and maybe two in his side or in his soft underbelly. Then we close in with our swords and cut him down. We'll soon have his ugly head mounted on our wall."

"That Lancelot!" muttered Queen Isabel.

"And then, I promise you, we'll have one more quest, the destruction of the cheese fiend, to boast about as we feast here at the Round Table on winter nights."

"Thank you, Sir Lancelot," Giraffe replied. "Your

plan stirs the blood. But does King Arthur want the head of his chief cook's son mounted on the wall of his banqueting chamber?"

"No, Giraffe,"said the king. "That would ruin the peace and the society I have labored to establish here. A war with the dragons, which would surely follow, is too dreadful to contemplate. But what do you propose? We don't want the head of our cook's son mounted here as a trophy; but neither do we want it spouting fire and gorging itself on our cheese and bananas."

"I understand, your majesty. And so I say again, I need a very small knight to complete this quest, but a knight who is also strong and brave."

"Do you want Sir Dinadan, Giraffe?" asked Queen Isabel with a smile. "If any knight of the Round Table is small, he is. But are you brave, Sir Dinadan?"

At this question, the whole Round Table roared with mirth.

"I am, your majesty," Sir Dinadan proclaimed as the laughter subsided. "I am if Giraffe decides I am."

"I do," Giraffe announced solemnly so everyone would hear and believe. "I do, and I choose you, Sir Dinadan, to accompany me on this quest."

"I won't argue with you, Giraffe," said King Arthur. "I can see you have made your choice. And Sir Dinadan, although we sometimes mock him and, indeed, although he sometimes mocks himself, I have found to be a brave knight—too brave for his own good sometimes—and surprisingly strong for his size, especially in his hands and arms.

"But tell me, Giraffe," the king continued, "what is

the nature of this quest, for which you find Sir Dinadan especially suited?"

"Pardon me, your majesty," Giraffe requested, "please allow Sir Dinadan to describe his quest to you and the queen and the Round Table after he has accomplished it."

"Very well, Giraffe," the king responded with a smile, which he directed chiefly toward his queen. "Isabel and I give you our confidence. Do what you think is required to remove this scourge from Camelot and to save the kingdom. But surely we can provide you and Sir Dinadan some gear or some assistance?"

"Yes, your majesty, Sir Dinadan and I will need at least two kinds of support. First, from your famous blacksmith, Vulcan, the glow of whose forge I saw as the queen and I walked over here from the station."

"Of course," said the king, "Vulcan makes the best swords and shields in Montana—although I'm not sure he can make them dragon-proof. He also creates fine, close-fitting chain mail and armor—greaves, breastplates, gloves, beavers. Look at Sir Galahad's outfit: Vulcan forged that. He'll outfit Sir Dinadan in the best and latest style. And as for swords, he's hammered out the very sharpest and toughest—except, of course, for my own Excalibur."

"Thank you, your majesty, but Sir Dinadan had best outfit himself in Scottish wool and a comfortable pair of Montana moccasins. What he needs from Vulcan is a good pair of tongs."

"Tongs, Giraffe?" Sir Lancelot hooted. "Do you plan to pinch the dragon to death?"

"That Lancelot!" muttered the queen.

"If Giraffe arms me with tongs," proclaimed Sir Dinadan above the laughter that followed Lancelot's mockery, "I'll go into battle with tongs."

"Very well, Sir Knight, very well," the king said as he attempted to choke down his own amusement. "And what, Giraffe, is the second form of support you and Sir Dinadan require?"

"That I will determine, Sire, if I may, in private counsel with Queen Isabel."

✠ ✠ ✠

"How can I aid Sir Dinadan in his quest, Giraffe?" the queen asked her old friend. They were alone in the royal parlor.

"In your capacity as a doctor, Queen Isabel."

"As a doctor? To treat his wounds and burns?"

"I hope not. I understand you are furnishing a clinic here in Camelot, as you did in your father's kingdom, to treat knights and dragons and all of King Arthur's subjects."

"That's true, Giraffe. I'm still waiting for Billy the Beaver to deliver my x-ray equipment, my MRI tube, and my dragon scan; but I've made a start."

"Nectarine told me you'd removed a cyst from her neck, and you are planning somewhat more invasive procedures to treat other dragons in the realm, is that true?"

"Yes, Giraffe, I'm trying to treat all of Arthur's subjects. But honestly, it's proving more difficult than I expected. There are plenty of books on the anatomy of beavers and raccoons and even crocodiles. But on dragons, Giraffe, there is hardly a thing. The king and I spent our honeymoon in Chicago so I could use the university library, a very great library indeed. And the medical librarians there were tremendously generous and helpful. But we couldn't find anything relevant except a medieval acccount of dragon's breath. That was instructive as far as it went—I now understand the fire glands of dragons better than anyone in the modern world. But I've had to pick up the rest by trial and error. I've still got a long way to go."

"But, Dr. Isabel, you have had occasion to employ anesthesia on your dragon population, haven't you?"

"Yes, several occasions. But I've had problems. I started with ether, using it on Cauliflower Vegetable, who needed what some people call a 'nose job.' You chuckle, Giraffe, but if you had seen her before—"

"Actually, your majesty, I've had an account."

"She was really pitiful, and I couldn't turn her down although, as I explained to her, I didn't really know what effect ether might have. I didn't have much of a sense of feminine beauty either, not as dragons understand it. But she was determined. 'Just look at this snout, doctor—I mean, your majesty—just look,' she said. 'Charlton could never love a snout like this.' Charlton, who was just an oafish Fruit to me then, was the object of her affections. I couldn't turn her down, could I?"

"No, your majesty—I mean, doctor—I'm sure you were right to operate."

"But not to use ether, Giraffe. Ether, as my nurse, Katie the raccoon, discovered, stimulates a dragon's fire glands. Cauliflower had just gone under and we were about to proceed—I had my scalpel at her nose—when her chest heaved and she exhaled a stream of fire that scorched the ceiling of the operating room. Luckily, Katie and I were clad in our asbestos gowns, or we might have been incinerated right then and there."

"I can see," Giraffe observed thoughtfully, "ether will not be appropriate to Sir Dinadan's quest. But have you found any safe anesthesia for dragons, your majesty?"

"I made several tries with intravenous chemicals, Giraffe, but dragon skin is so tough I couldn't make a needle penetrate except in the wing, and the fluid simply wouldn't flow or circulate adequately. Finally, I tried what I should have started with, chloroform. That works."

"Good, your majesty," Giraffe exclaimed with relief. "Could you fill me an aerosol spray can with chloroform?"

"No, Giraffe," Queen Isabel replied with some severity. "Aerosol ruins the environment. But I could fill an old-fashioned spray gun with a hand pump, if that will serve your turn."

"Yes, doctor, a hand-operated spray gun filled with chloroform is precisely what Sir Dinadan will need for his quest."

✠ ✠ ✠

Sir Dinadan was gently pricking o'er the plain. Actually, Sir Dinadan, who was trying his best to ride this giraffe as a knight would ride his horse, and Mango, who was perched comfortably between Giraffe's horns, had left the plain behind some time ago. Now the three of them climbed through heavily tangled brush and thorn trees and felt their way up the rugged slope of a small mountain. Mango guided.

She visited her brother every few days in a cave high up in the gnarled face of this mountain, as she had admitted to Giraffe.

"He'll be asleep," she told her companions. "He sleeps during the day. He's in so much pain, he hasn't left his cave in three days."

"We will approach him very carefully," said Giraffe. "Warn me to halt when we get close."

"What's the use of this spray gun, Giraffe?" asked Sir Dinadan.

He wore the wool and the moccasins Giraffe had prescribed and carried the tongs, the spray gun, and a little backpack slung across his shoulder. He had discovered a convenient dip in Giraffe's back and rode along quite comfortably.

"I can guess what I must do with the tongs, but why the spray gun?"

"All in good time, Sir Dinadan, as King Arthur might say. Don't forget, Mango," he said, "to stop us before we get within earshot—not to say flameshot—of Charlton's cave."

"Here," said Mango after the little party had climbed for a few more minutes. "This is a good place to stop, Giraffe. The cave lies just beyond that great sooty boulder."

"Good," said Giraffe. "Let's pause here to make ourselves ready. Dismount, Sir Dinadan, and open the pack."

The pack, about which Giraffe had been quite secretive when he was loading Sir Dinadan for this adventure, contained a miner's cap with a lamp in the front—no steel helmet—an asbestos suit—no steel armor—and a gas mask. The asbestos suit had been an afterthought of Dr. Isabel—a very good one, as it would turn out; the miner's cap and the gas mask Giraffe had borrowed from the Camelot Historical Museum.

"This is peculiar equipment for a knightly quest," Sir Dinadan remarked as he pulled these things out of the pack.

"True, Sir Knight," Giraffe admitted, "but this is a peculiar quest and, I must tell you, a very dangerous one. Are you resolved to carry it out?"

"Yes, Giraffe. If you will direct me, I am resolved."

And the little knight drew himself up to his full height.

As Sir Dinadan donned this knightly gear with the help of Mango, who acted as his squire, securing the ankles of the suit and tightening the mask, Giraffe explained to him what he had to do.

"You must walk quietly, carrying the spray can, to the open mouth of the cave and the open mouth of the dragon. Then you must spray this magic fluid directly into Charlton's nostrils, five sprays and no more, according to the instructions of Queen Isabel, into each nostril."

"No more than five, remember," Mango whispered.

"Then," Giraffe continued, "while we wait a few minutes for the spray to take effect, Sir Dinadan, bring the spray can back to me and exchange it for the tongs."

"Okay," said the knight. "That seems an easy enough quest."

"Yes," said Giraffe, "that should be quite easy. Then," he continued, "you must climb down the dragon's throat and extract his infected tooth."

"Right into the dragon's mouth, Giraffe?"

"Yes, Sir Dinadan, into his mouth and down his throat. And don't forget the tongs. Are you having second thoughts?"

"No, Giraffe, I'm ready. Just tell me what you want me to do."

"After you become sure of your footing, proceed down the throat. Be careful, the tongue may be slippery, especially if you find a little banana oil on it. Then as you push into the dark—and not before—click on the miner's lamp."

Giraffe turned toward Charlton's little sister. "Tell me, Mango,where will Sir Dinadan find the bad molar?"

"It's on the left; it's on the left, Sir Dinadan, Charlton's left. No wait. It will be on your right as you go down his throat. Do you know what I mean?"

"Yes, I understand perfectly, Mango."

"Really, Sir Dinadan," the little dragon assured him, "you won't be able to miss it if you aim your lamp. Charlton's gum is so red and swollen. You will be gentle with my poor brother, won't you?"

"Yes, my dear, as gentle as I can be."

"Once you reach the bad tooth," Giraffe continued, "you should kneel and, as carefully as possible, attach the tongs."

"And then, Giraffe?"

"And then," Giraffe replied, "one quick wrench

should do it. That's better, I believe, than teasing the molar out of the gum. Yes, Sir Dinadan, one determined wrench, and you will have accomplished your quest."

"And then what, Giraffe?" asked the knight with a shudder. "Do you think Charlton will lie still for that? "

"I can't say," Giraffe admitted. "The chloroform, the pain, the surprise. You know the patient better than anyone else, Mango. What do you expect him to do when Sir Dinadan assaults his tooth?"

"I'm not sure, Giraffe. When Charlton finds a strange knight lurking in his gullet, and when he feels the awful tug on his sore gum?"

"You must be prepared for anything, Sir Dinadan," Giraffe advised his chosen knight.

"To be chewed and swallowed?"

"I hope not," Giraffe responded uncertainly. "You need not continue in this quest, Sir Knight. It is perilous."

"I'm ready, Giraffe, ready for anything. I will extract your brother's tooth, Mango, no matter what follows."

"Is there anything you should tell Sir Dinadan, Mango, to help him prepare for this quest?"

"I can't think of anything, Giraffe. Oh, yes. Charlton does have a friend here in the mountains, Rolf, the flying fox. He cleans the bits of cheese and banana from Charlton's teeth. But he only shows up at the end of the night after Charlton comes back from his meals."

"Do he and Charlton talk to one another?" Giraffe asked.

"Not much. When he appears, swooping down from a tree, he just says, in that squeaky little voice of his—Rolf is really a bat, Giraffe"—and here Mango imitated Rolf—"'It's me, Charlton, your friend, Rolf; I've come to clean your teeth.' Actually he's come to get himself a treat. That bat loves banana. Then he works his way around Charlton's mouth and down his throat, avoiding the sore gum, of course. But I'm sure he won't come this morning, Sir Dinadan."

"Is there anything else, Mango?" Giraffe asked. "Think hard."

"No, Giraffe, that's it."

"Are you ready now, Sir Dinadan?" Giraffe asked his knight.

"I'm ready," Sir Dinadan replied as he grasped the spray can and vanished around the boulder.

✠ ✠ ✠

At first, the operation proceeded according to plan. Sir Dinadan, after administering Charlton five squirts of chloroform and then five more, reappeared around the boulder. Mango, Sir Dinadan, and Giraffe, all three, waited for a few minutes, listening for sounds of heavy breathing and relaxation, which they agreed after a little while they had started to hear. Cautiously, they all circled the boulder, approached the patient's gaping mouth, and confirmed his deep, motionless sleep. Sir Dinadan took the tongs from Giraffe, hoisted them carefully on his shoulder, climbed over Charlton's lower lip, which seemed to be completely relaxed, and into the dragon's mouth.

The brave little knight stretched one of his legs between Charlton's front teeth, swung the other up and over, and set his foot on the tongue. As Giraffe had warned him, it proved slippery. But Sir Dinadan was agile, and by using one of Charlton's teeth for leverage, he was able to pull himself over the dragon's lip and, despite the aromatic film of banana, stand steady inside his mouth.

"I'm glad I'm wearing these moccasins and not steel shoes," he said to himself.

Then he looked down at Giraffe, who crouched as low as he could to the side of the patient, and at Mango, who stood on tiptoe in front and peered in; and he gave them a high sign.

He turned then and proceeded gently along the tongue, keeping to the center, and, after a few steps, climbed out of view of his companions down the throat. Soon, however, Giraffe and Mango saw the miner's lamp reflecting from Charlton's palate, and that relieved them.

Sir Dinadan, who had rejected the gas mask— "It's much too big for me, Giraffe"—did not, even as he went deeper and deeper, find the scent of cheese and bananas overwhelming.

"I suppose Rolf has been here before me," he said to himself, "and cleaned up the place."

When Sir Dinadan had got part way down, however, he felt Charlton's tongue begin to twitch and swell, and the sharp tip of it reached down his throat, apparently in search of the intruder. Sir Dinadan stopped in his tracks so as not to tickle, he aimed his lamp down, and held his breath. The tip of Charlton's tongue reached further and further down until it almost touched the lamp.

Just before it touched, the knight spoke up and, in a voice imitating Mango imitating Rolf, he said, "It's me, Charlton, your friend, Rolf. I've come to clean your teeth."

Then he waited.

Gradually Charlton's tongue relaxed; and, after the dragon cleared his throat and belched, it slid gradually back to the front of his mouth.

Sir Dinadan stood in place for a moment to be sure all was quiet. Then he crept on, soon reaching the diseased molar, which seemed to be almost four inches across, and the swollen gum.

"Poor Charlton."

He affixed his tongs with great care.

"They are," he thought to himself as he worked, "barely wide enough."

Then he took a firm grasp of the handles, one handle with each of his hands, flexed his back and shoulders, and prepared to pull.

✠ ✠ ✠

Giraffe and Mango waited outside with great anxiety, especially when they heard what sounded to them like a swallow followed by a powerful belch emerging from deep in Charlton's throat. After they saw the tip of the tongue return to rest, they listened breathlessly and realized, as seconds passed, the cave's mouth and the dragon's mouth were completely silent.

"I have tried to do more," Giraffe thought to himself, "than I could do; and I have sent a gallant knight to his death."

Mango was beginning to smoke and sob.

Suddenly, the whole cave seemed to shudder. A strange noise rumbled up from the sleeping dragon's belly, a digestive noise that made the gray hair on Giraffe's head stand on end and his horns twitch.

After a brief stillness in the air, a heavy fume of rotten banana began to rise from the dragon's gaping mouth and fill the cave. Then, with an explosive flash, a tremendous flame surged in horrid, sizzling waves, wave after wave, from his throat. And on one of these waves, bearing a massive molar in his triumphant tongs, came Sir Dinadan, surfing out of the dragon's mouth and landing at the mouth of the cave, upright between his terrified companions.

Queen Isabella

✠ ✠ ✠

"Thank you, Giraffe," King Cole said to his friend, who had plumped the old king's pillow. "That will do all a pillow can do.

"I'm happy," the king continued, "you braved what I hear is terrible weather to pay me this visit. I have several topics I need to discuss."

"Please tell me what I can do, your majesty."

"First of all, Giraffe, describe the preparations people are making for Christmas at Friendship Hall. Although I will not be with you this year, neither the queen nor I, I am anxious the celebration should not suffer. Tell me, Giraffe, has the tree been installed?"

"We chose a royal spruce this year, your majesty, as a memorial to the Queen. Zane and Zack hauled it over Naval Point to the hall, and Ella, with a little help from Balleau and me, fixed it in place. I'm afraid Ella got a needle or two stuck in her trunk, but Dr. Isabel—I should say Queen Isabel, shouldn't I?—who traveled over from eastern Montana to enjoy the installation, was able to extract them without causing Ella as much pain as she had expected.

"It is a lovely tree, your majesty, and its aroma fills the hall. It is not as big nor as grand as Peter o'Possum's great pine, of course, but the beavers erected a stand that allows it to tower too tall almost for me to reach the top—that is, without a ladder—in the middle of the hall."

"Is it big enough," the king asked, "to hold all our lights and ornaments?"

"No, your majesty, not quite all; but we have draped our festoons of popcorn and old socks and sashes and paper chains around the walls and illuminated them with the lights that look like candles; we've nailed the zebras' antlers over the doors; and the tree, which we're ready to decorate, should support the rest of our collection."

"Is Hal going to direct the lights?" asked the king. "He won't have to do much climbing if you and the possums assist him."

"I met him trudging over to the hall, your majesty, as I was coming to visit you; and the possums, who've been serving in the Montana Air Force, have already assembled there. They are looking forward to the climb around our tree, Percy tells me, the way Billy the beaver looks forward to a holiday ride on a train."

"Good, Giraffe, good. There must also be presents and wassail—lots of wassail. And there must be singing; I guess it's too late to call down to Tennessee for my fiddlers three."

"Carolers are practicing at the hall this very afternoon, your majesty; Catherine the cook is stirring a batch of wassail in the palace kitchen even as we speak; and Oscar the footman has already washed out the vats from last Christmas. We'll be ready for the great day, have no fear."

"That's one worry off my mind. But what about Casper the crocodile and Allison the alligator? I hope this freezing weather doesn't make them too stiff or sleepy to attend. Everybody should come, Giraffe, everybody who can."

"The pond has not yet frozen, and I saw Allison and Casper this morning exercising beside it in their determination to remain flexible and wakeful enough to attend our party. Moreover, your majesty, according to Dr. Neil, the weather will moderate between now and Christmas."

"Good, Giraffe, good. We must fill Friendship Hall with revelers, as we did last Christmas."

"That is our intention," Giraffe said, bending his head toward the king. "What next, your majesty? I believe you had another concern."

"My daughter, Giraffe, the Princess Isabel."

"I stand ready to help her," Giraffe asserted, "any way I can."

"Of course, of course, Giraffe, but I have a couple of special concerns about her. First, her name."

"Her name, your majesty?"

"Yes. Ever since her sister married King Arthur and became Queen Isabel—an alliance I strongly supported, as you know—I've felt the princess should change her name. We shouldn't have two Queen Isabels of Montana."

"But to change the princess's name, especially when she herself rejected such a step, if your majesty remembers, would surely upset her—and others as well."

"True, Giraffe, true," the king acknowledged. "I also remember the trouble we had in naming her, her mother and I. And even though her mother is dead, I see several problems changing her name may cause. Rudolph's revolution strengthened my anxiety about this, Giraffe, as you no doubt understand. But I believe the need to avoid two Queen Isabels and the confusion that would cause justifies my decision."

"Do you recollect the problems that arose, your majesty, when the twins were born?"

"How could I forget, Giraffe? The queen fancied romantic names like Alexander and Cleopatra and Genghis and Aphrodite and Tomika and Hannibal. Yes, Giraffe, although she may have been ashamed to tell you about it, she had a real weakness for Hannibal, for Hannibal, Giraffe—think about it. On the other hand, I preferred simple English names like Rudolph, Bo Bo, Zane, Ella, Hal, Fergus, Gloria, Balleau, Kanga. You remember the arguments she and I had over this, don't you?"

"Only too well, your majesty."

"The only name the queen and I agreed on was the girl's name, Isabel. It was traditional enough for me and grand enough to suit her.

"I can hardly describe the pleasure, the relief, we both felt," the king continued after a pause, "when the queen produced a girl."

"No need to, your majesty. I will never forget that moment. You tied a purple ribbon around the baby's ankle, and then, as Dr. Oscar the orangutan held her up, you proclaimed, 'Welcome, Princess Isabel, undoubted heir of the middle of Montana.'"

"That was a happy moment, Giraffe. But it didn't last, did it?"

"No, your majesty, it seems Dr. Oscar had overlooked something."

"He overlooked something all right! The princess's twin. We did not have time even to start celebrating—not a minute—before my dear queen went back into labor.

"'What's the matter, darling?' I said. 'You can relax now; our Isabel is born.'

"'No, no,' the queen replied. 'I feel another baby coming.'

"'Another baby?' I cried. 'Dr. Oscar, what is happening?'

"But you remember all this, Giraffe, you were there."

"Yes, your majesty, and the second daughter, who came into the world bawling like a buffalo, was just as pretty and strong as the first one."

"I have remembered until my dying day, Giraffe, your presence of mind at the moment she emerged. I was speechless and actually unable to move, but you bent down over that second child as Dr. Oscar, who was almost as shocked as me, held her up to view, and pronounced, 'Isabel, our second Isabel. What wonderful luck for Montana; we have two heirs, two Isabels.'

"And the years that followed proved you right. Two Isabels. The queen and I and all Montanans have been, not only blessed, but doubly blessed.

"But times change, Giraffe," the king asserted with a change in his voice, "and they present us with different situations, different challenges. Two Isabels will soon be one Isabel too many.

"I'm not commanding a total change, however, only an embellishment."

"An embellishment, your majesty? I don't think I understand."

"Isabella, Giraffe, Isabella."

And the king began to sing, in a dry, wavering voice, "Bring a torch, Jeanette Isabella, bring a torch and tell everyone."

As he sang, he beat the time feebly with his right hand on the soft, white counterpane.

"Isabella?" Giraffe asked.

"Yes, my friend," the king assured him. "A little

Spanish embellishment, you see. When the princess is elevated—and that won't be long—there will be a Queen Isabel of eastern Montana and a Queen Isabella of middle Montana. I hope, Giraffe, you will help the princess understand why this change is necessary. Once again, I am depending on you."

"Yes, your majesty," Giraffe assured the dying king. "If it is your royal command, I will help Isabella adjust."

"Thank you," said the king.

Then after a little fit of coughing, he whispered hoarsely to his friend, "I'm tired, very tired, Giraffe, and I need a nap, but there is one more matter, a very important one, I wish to settle—if I can.

"Please fetch me a bowl of wassail while I snooze, and then, when you wake me with this refreshment, perhaps we can talk again. No hookah, don't bring me my hookah, Giraffe, I never took to that; just a nice steaming bowl of wassail."

✠ ✠ ✠

Giraffe had closed the door behind himself and left the king in a doze when Princess Isabel, who had been waiting in the hallway outside the sick room, addressed him through a wreath of condensation.

"Can you speak with me for a minute, Giraffe? There's a little something, actually something important, I need to ask you."

"Surely, your highness," Giraffe replied through a misty wreath of his own. He wondered why the king kept the castle so cold. It couldn't be the cost of electricity: everyone knew he had a lot of idle money.

Giraffe and the princess made their way down the cold cloister toward the small unheated council chamber, which she shared with her assistant, Fergus the footman's son, as the central office for the Montana Air Force.

"Patrick o'Possum," she said as they scurried along, "has flown Rebecca the raccoon up to Northport with him on a kind of a date. 'Young love,' Fergus calls it, and I can understand that—only too well. But it leaves us without a pilot for the flight to Camelot. This is not the first date of this kind, Giraffe. The foxes, who are waiting in the post office at Friendship Hall, have complained to Fergus for the last several days about the Air Force's deliveries. This is the Christmas season after all."

At that moment, her assistant raced toward them, puffing heroic wreaths as he came.

"Are you following me, Fergus?" the princess asked.

"No, your highness," he said apologetically. "I have a report."

"Well," said the princess, rubbing her hands together, "quit staring and report."

"A cat can look at a king, Princess Isabel," said Giraffe with a smile.

"Yes," she retorted, "and a cat can frighten a little mouse under a chair. But do you think Fergus could frighten a little mouse, Giraffe?"

"He might," Giraffe countered, "especially if he continues to hide his head in smoke."

"Well, Fergus, come out of hiding and report."

"Yes, your highness. We face worse problems every minute."

"Did you send the e-mail to Rudolf the red-nosed reindeer," said the princess, "as I asked you to do?"

"No, your highness," Fergus admitted.

"Why not? Do I have to do everything around here?"

"The blizzard that hit Northport is moving south," he explained, "and by now, I'm afraid the whole state is snowed in. I didn't think Rudolf could help us."

"I see," she responded. "Yes, I guess that's right. I'm sorry I mocked you, Fergus. You've done all you could—as usual. If the state is snowed in, the foxes will have to wait—and so will everybody else.

"But what's this worsening problem, then, Fergus? Fergus was the one, Giraffe, who came up with the notion to contact Rudolf the red-nosed reindeer. He went to Harvard, you know."

"Yes, I did," Fergus admitted, trying to hide his embarrassment. "That is, I did have such a notion. But now, it seems, there's nothing Rudolf can do. However, Marvin the mole, who dug his way over from Friendship Hall, has informed me of another problem."

"Oh, yes," the princess responded, "the worsening problem."

"Actually," Fergus replied, "a very different one. A number of Montanans beside Fred and Felicia, mostly raccoons and possums, who spent the afternoon in Friendship Hall decorating the tree and practicing carols, have been snowed in down there along with Hal the hippo and Gloria the gorilla, who has a beautiful soprano voice. And they don't have anything to eat or drink."

"I hope the hall is warm," said Giraffe. "I know it can resist the weather."

"Yes," Fergus assured him. "Marvin says the heatrola, which the king installed last fall, is roaring away, making things quite cozy, at least for those who huddle near it, and there are plenty of logs. But all the people, especially the younger ones, are getting very hungry, Marvin says."

"What can we do, Giraffe?" the princess asked. "Most of those carolers are children. We can't let them go without supper and breakfast. Who knows how long they'll be snowbound?"

"That's right, your highness," Giraffe replied. "Do you have an idea, Fergus? Did Harvard prepare you for such an emergency?"

"We have a supply of bread and honey," Fergus said, "that Catherine the cook has been storing for the winter. But of course the bread and honey are at the palace, and the hall is down at the point."

"Bread and mead," Giraffe insisted. "Fresh bread and hot mead. That's what the children require."

"Catherine and I can make mead from the honey," the princess suggested. "But how can we deliver it to the hall through this terrible blizzard?"

"There might be a way, your highness," Fergus said, looking up at Giraffe.

"There is a way," Giraffe agreed. "I must carry the bread and mead over to Friendship Hall, isn't that right, Fergus?"

"It doesn't take a Harvard education, Giraffe, to see you have the legs for the job."

"No, Fergus; no, Giraffe," the princess exclaimed. "Giraffe is a tropical creature, Fergus. He can't go out in conditions like this. I won't allow it."

"Your highness," Giraffe interrupted, "you forget I am a Montanan. A little snow doesn't frighten me, not anymore. Besides, if you look closely, you will notice I'm wearing the warm coveralls you gave me a few Christmases ago. Fergus is right. I am the person for the job, the only person."

"But Giraffe," the princess protested, "if you don't freeze, you'll get lost in the snow—and then what will I do? Besides, how can you carry enough mead and enough bread—with your tongue?"

"Fergus and his father must make me a harness so I can carry a vat of mead and a big basket of bread in one load. Time is wasting, Fergus, and I must set off while it is still light."

"I suppose you are right, Giraffe," said the princess. "We must supply our people who are snowbound in Friendship Hall—if you think you can do it."

"I can do it," Giraffe replied, "if you and Fergus will help me."

"Very well, then," said the princess, "since that is the agreement, let's get started.

"While you and your father are making a harness, Fergus, I will collect the bread and honey, and Catherine will help me brew the mead. Then we will fill one of the king's Christmas vats and balance it across Giraffe's back with a satchel of bread. Does that seem like a good plan, Giraffe?"

"Yes, your highness. I will take a bowl of wassail to the king, as he asked me to do, and have another little visit with him while you two prepare the honey and the harness. Summon me when everything is ready, and you and Fergus can load me. Then I will set off for Friendship Hall."

"Well?" said the princess to Fergus, who was standing about as if he had more to say. "Off you go. I have a little something to take up with Giraffe."

✠ ✠ ✠

"A little something, your highness?" Giraffe asked as he and the princess watched Fergus march away from them down the hall.

"He's a fine young man," he murmured, "even if he did attend Harvard.

"A little something, your highness?" Giraffe repeated.

"Yes, Giraffe," the princess replied, "a little something."

She drew a deep breath and exhaled an especially large wreath.

"I'm in love, Giraffe," she wailed, "hopelessly in love."

"Hopelessly, your highness?" Giraffe responded. "Why hopelessly?"

"Oh, Giraffe, he's the son of a footman. I've fallen for the son of a footman. Not only that, but he loves somebody else. What will people say, Giraffe? 'Princess Isabel was rejected by a footman's son.' What can I do?"

"Do you know he loves somebody else? Have you spoken to him?"

"No, Giraffe," she said pitifully and exhaled a great barrage of wreaths. "How could I? But I know she left him a letter when she ran off to join the circus. He showed it to me. Oh, Giraffe, it's Fergus I'm talking about, Fergus and Marian the maid."

"Tell me about the letter."

"Marian the maid wrote Fergus she was tired of dealing with all the bread and honey—not to speak of the laundry—now that Mother, I mean the queen, was dead. The manager of the circus recently offered her a wonderful position as Gilda, the girl with the removable nose. She had always wanted to be in show business, she admitted, and she couldn't pass up this opportunity. It was a replacement job—Fida, the dog-faced girl, had eloped with Hugo, the human garbage can—but there was a good chance for advancement.

"I tried to be sympathetic as I read this letter, Giraffe, but I couldn't help laughing—the human garbage can; and when he saw me laughing, Fergus started laughing, too."

"He must not have been too upset," Giraffe suggested, "if he could laugh at Marian's letter. How has he acted since she left?"

"I don't know, Giraffe. He hangs around a lot waiting for me to tell him what to do."

"I noticed he stared at you, especially when you weren't looking."

"Yes," the princess admitted, "he stares, but why doesn't he say anything?"

"Why don't you?"

"Well, I am the princess."

"Exactly."

"Oh! Yes, I see what you mean. I want Fergus to run all the risks. And that's not the way love should be, is it? But even if he loves me, what can we do? I must—we must—have the king's open approval, if not his commendation, don't you agree? That's why I'm talking to you here in this cold public passageway while people starve in Friendship Hall, and you prepare to risk your life to save them, and daddy is dying. Oh, Giraffe, so much is happening all at once. Can you help me?"

"I will be glad to do what I can, your highness. I will speak to the king before I set off for the hall and see what he may feel about the relationship, which, if I understand you, you desire. It will be quite easy to urge Fergus's personal excellence and your affection."

"Thank you, Giraffe. You will make it possible for us."

"I will do what I can, Princess Isabel, but you and Fergus must make your own declarations and decisions. Your love for each other is your own business, my dear, and without that, nothing I do matters.

"But now," Giraffe said in another tone, "let us hurry to the kitchen. You have the big problem of furnishing bread and mead; and I must fetch a bowl of wassail for the king."

✠ ✠ ✠

Giraffe found the king dozing restlessly when he opened the door of the sick room to bring the bowl the king had called for. Catherine the cook had thoughtfully given Giraffe a bowl with a handle, around which he could easily wrap his tongue. Carrying it carefully so as not to spill, he approached the king's bed. He scraped his hoof on the floor to waken the royal invalid and then waited quietly until he was recognized.

"Giraffe, Giraffe," the king muttered as he came around. "Oh, you've brought the bowl I called for."

Then he raised himself painfully above the covers and turned his head so Giraffe could help him drink. Giraffe bent his neck down, holding the brimming bowl steady. As the rich aroma of its steaming contents filled the room, the king took two or three swallows.

"That's good," he said with satisfaction, "very good. It brings back many happy times. Thank you."

"You're welcome," Giraffe replied after carefully setting the bowl, which still contained a few sips, on the king's bedside table. "There was another topic I believe, your majesty, besides the princess's change of name, which you wished to discuss with me."

"Indeed, there is one more thing on my mind."

Giraffe stood attentively while the king breathed and gathered his strength.

"I have a dream, Giraffe, a dream," whispered the king.

"Yes, your majesty?" Giraffe responded after a few seconds of silence.

"I have a dream," the king continued in a stronger voice, "that after my death, Montana will be governed by King Fergus and Queen Isabella.

"I see you're horrified, Giraffe," the king said with a smile, "horrified I could neglect the established orders of society and politics and marry my daughter, the heir to my throne, to a commoner, the son of a footman!"

"No, your majesty, surprised, but not horrified."

"Is it not the privilege of power, Giraffe, to choose, to lead the way?"

"Yes, your majesty, in matters of state."

"Well, well, is the succession of my crown and my duty to Montana not a matter of state?"

"To a point, your majesty, but love and marriage, which make up a part of your dream, are personal concerns."

"True, Giraffe, but I would be remiss in this matter, about which I feel strongly, not to use all the power I have. And therefore, I have written and signed a proclamation, a proclamation to which I have also affixed my seal. Please read it and tell me how it strikes you."

The king then held forth a document, which Giraffe took with his tongue and carried over to a window. It read:

> *I, King Cole of Montana, being of sound mind, do command the marriage of my daughter, Princess Isabella of Montana, to Fergus macOscar and the consequent elevation of the said Fergus to joint eminence and power with his queen, the said Princess Isabella.*

"Well, Giraffe, what do you think?"

"I approve very heartily, your majesty. It is a clear and appropriate assertion of your authority—except for one letter."

"One letter, Giraffe, one alphabetical letter?"

"Yes, one letter. I advise your majesty to change an *a* to an *e* in the word 'command' as you use it in this proclamation."

"Command? Commend? 'I...commend.' Oh, Giraffe, your mother was a scorpion."

Nevertheless, he made the change Giraffe had suggested and, after examining his correction, he admitted, "That is better, I agree. Are they in love? Do they wish to marry one another?

"Actually," he said smugly, "I know the feelings of one of them. Yes, I know her feelings. When Fergus was loading a vat of wassail in our sled last Christmas, Giraffe, it slipped out of his hands, and wassail spilled all over the front steps of the palace.

"'Well, young man,' I said in annoyance, 'I see why Harvard never won a wrestling title.'

"I was wrong, I admit. He had not meant to drop my wassail; and the vat was heavy, especially in the cold weather. But I made him clean the steps.

"'We're not driving to the celebration,' I said, 'until those steps are clean and that vat has been refilled.'

"I wasn't going to run out of wassail, Giraffe.

"Well sir, before Fergus could start repairing the damage, Princess Isabel—my feisty young heir—hopped out of the sled, grabbed a mop and started to help him clean up. She was wearing her scarlet cloak, her ruby slippers, and a shimmering white dress that would have been easier to stain than the pink meringue she wore to Billings. But she didn't rest until the steps were clean, the vat was reloaded, and our sled was ready to leave. All the time, by the way, Marian the maid kept her seat and fingered her pretty nose to make sure it was on straight.

"Since then, I've kept my eyes open, and if ever I witnessed love in my long life, I saw it in my dear daughter. She dotes, Giraffe, she dotes on that young man."

"I believe that's true, your majesty; she confessed as much to me. She asked me to discuss her feelings with you, in fact, and to find out what chance there might be of your commending her love and their marriage."

"As you know, Giraffe, I do *commend* such a marriage. But how does the young man feel? That's the question. I know he fancied Marian the maid—once she had acquired her new nose. But does he still?"

"Marian the maid ran away a few days ago, your majesty, to join the circus. She accepted an offer to appear as Gilda, the girl with the removable nose. She left Fergus a letter, which he showed Princess Isabella. Marian explained that for the present, she would be a replacement for a couple of performers who had run away together."

"Good, good," said the king. "That takes care of Marian. But where does it leave my daughter?"

"Fergus and the princess laughed together over the letter, your majesty, or at least, as she has told me, over the circus romance that gave Marian her chance; and the young man shows other signs, which the princess herself has noticed, that his affections have changed direction. I suggested to her, however, she must be the one to speak."

"True, true, Giraffe, the princess must speak first."

There was a knock at the door.

"I must leave now, your majesty, with your permission, and take a hike over to Friendship Hall. The carolers, about whom I told you, have become snowbound, as we have just learned. Fergus and the princess are collecting bread and mead that are sorely needed over there; and once they load me with these supplies, I will set off."

"One more act of friendship, Giraffe?"

"Everything I've ever done, I've done for friendship, your majesty, although I'm beginning to wonder if friendship will take us all the way."

"Not all the way, perhaps, my philosophical friend," the king responded, "not all the way. But it has taken you and me," he said, lifting his head off his pillow, "as far as we can go."

Giraffe nodded, and after a pause, he spoke again. "I will return to the palace after making my deliveries, your majesty, and if I detect any progress in the romantic negotiations you and I have discussed, I will come and tell you."

"Yes, please do. I do not have long to live, Giraffe, as Dr. Oscar has discovered. But I will die content if I can be sure I have left Montana in the care of Fergus and Isabella."

✠ ✠ ✠

"I wish we had a pack of St. Bernards for this job," said Fergus the footman's son as he tied the last rope of the harness around Giraffe's neck, "but I guess you'll have to do."

"If you can do, Giraffe," said the princess as she gave the rope a tug. "Are you sure about this? Fergus has really weighted you down. And look at the gray hair between your horns! You're too old for this. Don't you agree, Fergus? Giraffe is too old to carry such a load in such a blizzard."

"I suppose," Fergus responded, "we might postpone his excursion until spring."

"But then, I'll be even older," Giraffe said with a smile. "You mustn't worry, your highness, not about me, anyway. My old legs are strong, and the coveralls you gave me will keep me warm until I reach the hall."

"Are you planning to go on to your cave, Giraffe," the princess asked, "after you distribute the bread and mead?"

"No, Princess Isabel," he answered. "I believe I should return to the palace. I may be needed here."

"Oh, yes, Giraffe, I'm so glad you're coming back. You will be needed. Here," she cried as Giraffe plodded toward the door, "wear this scarf; it will help a little."

"No, my dear," Giraffe responded. He gave his neck a toss. "These coveralls give me all the warmth I need."

After opening the palace door, Fergus accompanied Giraffe a few steps toward Friendship Hall and, as they trudged along together, he expressed his agreement with the princess.

"I'm also glad you plan to return tonight, Giraffe. There's something very important I need to ask you."

"I can see," Giraffe thought to himself, "I'm going to be very busy tonight. But first I must carry this load over to the carolers—if my bad leg holds out."

That was a large order—"A large order of bread and

mead," Giraffe muttered as he surveyed the almost completely hidden way.

He had observed, when Fergus opened the door, the snow was drifting; and it had already climbed five or six feet up the palace wall. The pine trees, he noticed now, were so heavily laden their branches groaned and creaked; and, although it was only two o'clock in the afternoon, night seemed to be closing in. The wind was gusting. It was snowing, and it was going to snow.

He trudged toward the hall, striding at one step through a heavy bank of white and at the next across a slick patch of open ground. A white swath, he came to realize, might hide a slope or even a hole; and the step down into two or three feet of snow would always require a slippery climb back up to level ground. If he shifted his balance as he climbed, he was almost sure to fall. And even if he could get up again once he had tumbled, he would certainly lose his load. In fact, he would have to drop his load if he could—Fergus had secured it very firmly—in order to get up at all. His long legs helped while he kept upright, Giraffe came to understand. But getting them—especially his left hind leg—back under himself once he had fallen: that might not be possible. And for a moment he did feel old, old and lame and lost in snow.

Suddenly, Giraffe was overcome with fatigue. As he gazed over the deeply covered bed of the forest around him, he recollected the rich aroma of wassail—"Wassail," he said—and thought how pleasant it would be to lie down for a moment and let the wind cover him with its soft, white counterpane. He loved the wind as it whispered in his ears, tickled his horns and ruffled his hair; and the snow, which had seemed bitter when it was pelting his face, had become, as he paused to look around himself, smooth and inviting. Yes, he was old, as the princess had noticed, old and gray and tired; and it would be delicious to relax for a moment in the deep, beautiful snow.

"But, no," he said aloud.

He was needed, as Fergus had reminded him. The king needed his bowl of wassail, and the king's daughter needed her old friend's sympathy—and his counsel—at least until the new partnership of King Fergus and Queen Isabella had become established. And who would help the young queen adjust to her new name? Besides, the folks at Friendship Hall needed the bread and mead he was delivering, that no one but him could deliver. He remembered Gloria the gorilla was there and regretted he wasn't bringing her any banana punch.

"She'll just have to get by this time on mead," he murmured to himself.

And that cheered him. Yes, people were depending on him in both the palace and the hall. He could rest another time.

So Giraffe kept going. He lifted his great hooves at each step as little as he must to slog ahead. And he gradually developed a gait like a camel.

"Just like a camel," Giraffe thought to himself.

He scooted through the growing accumulation of snow, shoveling it to the side one step at a time as he went along. The light held, the grey light without lustre, and he soon found the old familiar way out onto Naval Point. Without losing a drop or dropping a loaf, he reached Friendship

Hall, the looming octagon in which his fellow Montanans were imprisoned.

As he approached its great eastern door, Giraffe heard an infant weeping and then the sweet coo of Patsy o'Possum chanting, "Hush, Quinella, hush my babe, momma is here."

He gave the door a kick. Gloria the gorilla, who had been on watch, swung it open, pushing aside, with much ado, the snow that had drifted up against it since Marvin the mole's departure. After he had stamped his hooves and shaken himself, Giraffe entered bearing his golden gifts.

✠ ✠ ✠

On the return trip, Giraffe left his harness at the hall, and Peter o'Possum, who went along to help him see the way, rode him bareback as he had often done before.

Hal the hippo, who had been surveying the tree and organizing the lights when the blizzard struck, asked to accompany them.

"I think it's right, Giraffe, let me tell you, I should be present at the palace on this occasion."

He trailed his friends through the deepening snow—but not by much. Hal was more nimble, as he reminded them from time to time while they trudged along, than most people realized. Suddenly, Giraffe realized he was nimble, too; his old legs felt fine; and the hike back to the palace, even in the growing darkness, was a bowl of wassail.

Fergus and Princess Isabel were waiting just inside the palace door when the hikers arrived.

"Oh, Giraffe," the princess exclaimed as Fergus forced back the snow and ushered him in, "Fergus and I were so anxious about you, weren't we Fergus?"

"You and Fergus?" Giraffe said curiously as he examined the two of them.

Their eyes gleamed with a greater happiness, he noticed, than his safe return could explain. Their faces glowed with an obviously shared delight; and their bodies radiated with energy and joy.

"Well, well," Giraffe thought to himself, "I will be able to bring glad tidings to the king."

"His majesty," Fergus announced, "is very eager to see you, Giraffe, if your trip has not exhausted you."

"Oh, yes," the princess said. "Daddy is very eager to talk with you."

"If you gentlemen will accompany us," said Fergus, addressing himself to Peter and Hal, "Princess Isabel and I will escort you to the great hall where a number of our friends are assembled. Catherine the cook and my father, Oscar the footman, have spread a small collation, which may refresh you after your hike."

✠ ✠ ✠

When Giraffe closed the door of the sick room behind him and straightened his neck, he observed with apprehension that the king, who was gazing up at him, looked exhausted.

"Yes, Giraffe," he said, "I have been extremely busy since you left. Leo has visited and shaken his snowy mane all over my counterpane; Ella stuck her trunk through the door and trumpeted her sympathy; and, of course, Dr. Oscar dropped by to look down my throat and feel my pulse. Both of the Oscars and Catherine, too, have been hovering over me with their kind attentions. They bustle so."

"I'm afraid all this excitement is bad for you, your majesty."

"Yes, Giraffe, but it no longer matters. I have also entertained the young lovers."

"The young lovers, your majesty? Then you have seen what has happened?"

"Yes, Giraffe. Who could miss it? It makes me very happy, very happy—but very tired. Could you help me to a few more sips of wassail? There are a few more sips in the bowl, I believe."

Giraffe wrapped his tongue around the handle of the bowl he had earlier left on the table. He tipped it carefully so King Cole could reach what little was left.

The king drank with some effort. "That's good, Giraffe, cold but good. I've always loved wassail. Thank you."

Suddenly, he started up in bed, almost shaking the empty bowl out of Giraffe's grasp.

"Don't call for my hookah," the king commanded. "I've never taken to that, Giraffe. Don't call for my hookah! But my fiddlers, my fiddlers. Yes, call for my fiddlers three!"

✠ ✠ ✠

A number of people had gathered in the great hall of the palace. Hal and Peter found, besides Dr. Oscar the orangutan, who had attended the king for the last few days, and Marvin the mole, who had carried the bad news from Friendship Hall, Ella and Leo and Kanga. Ella had slogged over, having heard from Giraffe the day before the king was near death, chiefly to express her sympathy for the princess; Leo had arrived earlier with a mane full of snow, having struggled to the palace, leaping and scrambling through the growing drifts, out of *noblesse oblige*—to pay the king his last respects; and Kanga had hopped over early, before the snow became heavy, to help Catherine with the household mead and the Christmas wassail. She had, of course, brought Roo with her. Queen Isabel, unfortunately, was snowbound with her husband, King Arthur, at Camelot in eastern Montana.

All the folks who were present in the great hall sampled the delicacies Catherine the cook had prepared for them. Dr. Oscar the orangutan, courtesy of Oscar the footman, who had gone to some trouble to procure fresh fruit, chose a piece or two from a tray; Leo the lion enjoyed a venison pie, a specialty of Catherine's; Kanga and Ella shared a nice plate of nuts. On a side table, Peter o'Possum found an elegant dish of live grubs only a few of which Marvin the mole had already eaten. And Hal the hippo, after an embarassing little delay, was served some newly thawed slime. Catherine gave Roo, the only child present, a little basket of Christmas candies.

"You may select two, and no more, Roo," said his mother, "until you've had your supper."

The assembly was solemn, but not depressed, and everybody had a story to tell. Ella, who hardly mentioned the discomfort she had suffered squeezing herself into the great hall, described to Kanga the spruce needles Queen Isabel had recently extracted from her trunk.

"The pain, Kanga, the pain: you can hardly imagine how sensitive my trunk is."

Kanga, in turn, explained to Ella, almost in a whisper, the argument over nutmeg and cinnamon she had had that morning with Catherine the cook.

"The king is very sick," Dr. Oscar confided to Leo, who slurped gravy, "but if he would just take this concentrate of banana punch I've prescribed—instead of that blasted wassail—I believe he would recover."

While Roo sneaked behind Hal to enjoy a third and then a fourth piece of fudge, the hippo and the possum shared with the mole an account of their trek over to the palace.

"The snow has got deeper since you found your way over here from Friendship Hall, Marvin," Hal asserted. "If you could see the drifts we plowed through, let me tell you, you wouldn't stick your pink nose above the ground until next spring."

Princess Isabel and Fergus the footman's son entered the hall, each of them carrying a pitcher and cups on a tray. At their signal, the cook and the footman, who had attended to the assembly's needs for some time, stepped aside. And the two young people circulated, making sure everyone was comfortable.

"May I pour you some hot chocolate?" the princess asked Peter o'Possum. "I bet you are still cold from your walk. Or would you prefer some of Kanga's famous mead? Fergus is pouring that."

The grace and generosity of the young couple as they attended to each of their guests, including Roo, who finally accepted a cup of chocolate at the princess's urging, produced a strange calm in the whole assembly.

"Aren't they sweet and gracious?" Ella confided to Kanga.

"And under such circumstances," her companion agreed.

Everyone finished his drink, set his cup on one of the trays, and waited.

After a moment, Giraffe entered the hall.

Its ceiling was sharply peaked so he was easily able, after taking a few measured steps, to stand at almost his full height. He carefully turned his head so he could see and acknowledge everyone present.

"Countrymen, Montanans, friends," Giraffe said in a muted but resonant voice, "King Cole is dead. Long live Queen Isabella!"

✠ ✠ ✠

The Wages of War

✠ ✠ ✠

Giraffe was limping alone down the path from the palace one beautiful spring day a few weeks after the coronation of Fergus and Isabella when he got a call on his cell phone. He wrapped his tongue around it, fastened it to his horns with the little hooks that had been attached to it for his convenience, and answered.

It was the dragon Persimmon, chief cook at King Arthur's castle, calling him from a pay phone down at the Camelot train station.

Giraffe's left hip was giving him a lot of grief these days, as Dr. Oscar the orangutan had predicted. He had wrenched it that morning on the way to the palace when he climbed up and down the steep bypath that led to King Cole's memorial. Afterwards, at the palace, he had shared what he realized might be his last farewell with the young king and queen—and suffered a different kind of grief.

So he had trouble at first paying his caller much attention. But Persimmon sounded so unhappy that, after a minute, Giraffe made himself listen more closely to what he was saying.

"We need your help again, Giraffe, Pine and I."

"Does Charlton have another infected tooth?" asked Giraffe. "I believe Sir Dinadan and Queen Isabel can take care of that."

"No, Giraffe, although he is himself again, Charlton does need a job. But it's our younger boy, Kumquat. And his problem is worse than Charlton's, much worse."

"Worse than Charlton's, Persimmon? That's hard to believe."

"You know, Giraffe, how difficult it is for a dragon, even a healthy, self-disciplined dragon, in polite society. He must manage his tail so as not to knock over lamps and vases and tumblers and goblets; he must take care not to rake his claws over the mahogany and walnut and cherry furniture—Queen Isabel is especially concerned about that; and, most important of all, he must govern his breath. I'm sure you understand this, Giraffe. With one flash of annoyance a dragon can terminate a friendship—or a friend. Even a cough or a sigh, if not adequately suppressed or not carefully directed, can singe a tapestry or a curtain, or ignite the beard of a companion—with unavoidable social consequences."

"Yes, yes," Giraffe responded a little impatiently, "but you parents simply have to raise your kids to observe these things."

"Pineapple and I have tried, Giraffe, we have tried with all our minds and hearts to instill in our three offspring the right way to conduct themselves—that is, to conduct themselves among other people. 'If you should become careless even for a second,' I have said to each of them I don't know how many times, 'if you are careless and turn your breath on one of the knights, especially if he is wearing his armor, you might very well roast him alive and be cast out of the castle forever.' Poor Charlton, as you know, Giraffe, is living proof of that. 'Eternal vigilance,' I have repeatedly told them, 'is absolutely necessary if you are to fulfill your mother's and my hopes for your personal success.'"

"I can see," said Giraffe, shifting his weight onto his good leg, "you have done all a parent can do. But what's the problem? Won't Kumquat learn these lessons?"

"He can't, Giraffe. Kumquat suffers from the worst illness that can afflict a dragon: he has hay fever."

"Oh," Giraffe responded, "that is serious. I thought you were going to complain about the name Pineapple saddled him with. I know how much you hate the name 'Kumquat' although I doubt it will prove to be a social or professional stumbling block."

"No, Giraffe, although I do hate his name, almost as much as Pineapple hates the name 'Charlton,' I know nothing can change it. But his hay fever, Giraffe, can't you help us with that? You cured Charlton."

"I don't know, my friend, nothing occurs. But King Arthur has recently commanded me to join him in Camelot, and if the king's problems are not severe, I'll try to visit you while I'm there. Meanwhile, I urge you to consult with Queen Isabel."

Giraffe did not feel as cheerful about this trip east as he had about the one last fall to save Camelot from Kumquat's brother. He had left the palace on this balmy spring morning hoping to creep back along the path toward his cave saying goodbye along the way to Kanga and Rudolph and, maybe, Peter o'Possum—dropping in later, perhaps, if his hip really began to hobble him, on Dr. Oscar.

The sun, which Giraffe could glimpse through the budding foliage of the trees, covered the floor of the forest beside his path with speckles of gold; and between the great dark trunks of pine and oak Giraffe could see the meadow and admire the pink and white and yellow of its fresh flowering.

"Zane and Zack will be cavorting today," he thought with a twinge of envy, "and Ella will be busy snatching the new clover."

He once believed he saw a patch of bluebonnets.

"But it's too far north for bluebonnets," he said to himself. "I wonder what flowers those blue ones are?"

He realized this was the season in which pollen made some people suffer, and he remembered his promised visit to Camelot.

Reluctantly, Giraffe turned down the path that led to the Montana railroad station.

✠ ✠ ✠

While they waited for Giraffe, Kumquat's parents talked things over. Instead of discussing their younger son's affliction, however, they poked the smoldering grounds of grievance—the way people do.

"Kumquat," said Persimmon to his wife after both Mango and Kumquat were safely in bed. "Why did you choose that name for him? As if he didn't already have enough troubles."

"Don't be so huffy, Sim. You know very well it's the second name of my favorite uncle."

"Oh, yes," her husband responded, stoking the fire, "your Chinese connection."

"At least he wasn't a paper dragon," Pineapple steamed, "like your famous grandfather, Uther. What a name that would have been for one of our poor boys."

She seethed with sarcasm.

"My grandfather, Uther Pendragon," Persimmon retorted heatedly, "rode on the tip of Arthur's spear when our king charged into battle; and he scorched all the fight out of those Saxon infidels."

"Why didn't you name Charlton 'Uther,' then," asked his wife with the slow burn that Persimmon had learned to fear, "if it's so heroic?"

"You know very well, my dear," he answered with a frigid diffidence he hoped might quench his wife's anger. "I'd seen Mr. Heston, who grimaces with a perfect dragon's profile, handle fire in his movies; I'd heard him really smoke the foes of firearms; and I just thought some of his heroism or some of his looks would ignite our son—or spark an example. I don't know. It seemed like a good idea at the time."

"Not to me, it didn't," fumed Pineapple with a crackle in her voice.

"It meant that you got to name our second boy, anyway," Persimmon recollected with a smoky wheeze. "Although if I'd known your choice—'Kumquat!'—I might not have given in so cooly."

"The names are okay," Pineapple said, simmering down a little, "if the boys didn't have such problems. Even now he's cured of his toothache, my dear Charlton can't find a job. Nobody wants him around the castle. And there's not a single knight who will give Kumquat the time of day. 'After all,' as Parsnip said to me over the rock pile yesterday, 'who's going to take a chance on a dragon with hay fever?' I hate that Parsnip."

"But she's right, my dear. Nobody at the castle wants to trust our son, and trust is an essential basis of friendship or employment. Nobody can trust Kumquat not to sneeze."

"When Vulcan took him as an apprentice over at the forge," Pineapple sighed, "I was so grateful. I had such a hot feeling here in my heart. He surely threw cold water on my hopes."

"That's not fair, Pine," Persimmon replied with a smoky sigh of his own. "Vulcan did his best to work with our boy. He got his gloves especially lined with asbestos and bought himself an asbestos kilt so he and Kumquat could work at the forge together."

"Well," Pineapple flared up, "he should have worn asbestos knickers."

A couple of scalding tears flowed down her jaw.

"Even after Kumquat singed him during their work a time or two," Persimmon continued, "Vulcan kept him on, trying to show him how to forge all the knightly equipment. I examined some of the things, a helmet and a lance and a sword, they made together. He and Kumquat also collaborated on this nice grill—it's just like the one at the castle only smaller. Kumquat had a gift for iron, Vulcan once told me as he and I discussed our boy over Vulcan's anvil, a real gift. And he did his best to nurture our youngster—as you well know."

"That's true," Pineapple admitted, trying to extinguish her tears. "But I can't forget the day Kumquat came home and told me he had misfired—"

"He had misfired *again,*" Persimmon corrected his wife.

"You must stop sobbing, Pine," he murmured, "or you'll ignite the rug.

"You remember he had already seared Vulcan's elbow once and, later, burned his nose. And both times Vulcan had forgiven him. 'It was just an accident,' he said the first time. 'I shouldn't have raised the hammer the way I did without warning young Kumquat.' He even overlooked the great blisters on his nose."

"I know," Pineapple acknowledged with a gulp. "Vulcan's nose did look a sight with those blisters. It was as swollen as that snout of Cauliflower's. I almost burst out laughing the first time I saw it. But it was painful, I could see that; and I was so happy when Vulcan forgave our boy."

"The third time, when Kumquat sneezed on Vulcan's knee and thigh, he just couldn't overlook it. As Vulcan said to me, 'It's not a question of forgiveness anymore, Persimmon, my friend: it's a matter of self-preservation.' And he still limps around his forge to this day. 'I'm fond of your son,' Vulcan said to me. 'He's a fine young person and a promising smith, but working around him is simply too dangerous.'

"I don't remember whether I told you or not, Pine, but Dr. Oscar the orangutan, who traveled over from the middle of Montana to inspect Vulcan's leg, is afraid he may never enjoy the full use of it again."

"I know," Pineapple cried as cold flashes shook her scales from her teeth to the tip of her tail. "But what can we do? Our poor child. When he sneezes, especially when he suffers a sneezing fit, it gets almost too hot and smoky in our cave even for me. And the walls become so sooty, I can hardly get them clean. Little Mango sobs and smokes so much whenever Kumquat has one of his attacks it almost melts my heart. And Kumquat doesn't want to sneeze, Persimmon, he can't help himself. What are we going to do?"

"I don't know, my darling," Persimmon said as he tried to stamp out the tears of his overheated wife. "I only hope Giraffe can help us."

✠ ✠ ✠

The first thing Giraffe did after he had descended from the train at Camelot was to pay a visit to Vulcan, about whose relationship with Kumquat he had learned from Dr. Oscar the orangutan. He found Vulcan busily forging equipment for King Arthur's next campaign.

"The Survivalists, as they call themselves," Vulcan informed him, "have been raiding the king's outposts all winter. They ride up from Colorado on what they call buckskins, they ransack the homes of Arthur's subjects, and drive off the cattle. When Unferth, one of the foremen on Arthur's range, threatened the last raiders with the king's vengeance, they laughed in his face and told him to scoot back to Camelot and tell Arthur they were waiting."

"What has the king done, Vulcan?" Giraffe asked over the bang, bang, bang of Vulcan's hammer.

"A few weeks ago, when the snow had melted, he dispatched Sir Lancelot and a small band of fully armored knights south to scout the situation."

"Lancelot boasts a little too much," Giraffe said, "but he is a brave knight, and, if he was accompanied by Galahad and Gawain, they must have been impressive. Did they find the Survivalists?"

"Yes, Giraffe," Vulcan replied, "they found them. But the Survivalists had guns—pistols and a couple of rifles; and the knights, even with the best armor and the best lances I could forge, were no match. Sir Lancelot returned with the great dent in his breastplate I'm trying now to repair and a terrible bruise on his chest; and the whole troop was routed and chased back to Camelot."

"What now?" Giraffe asked anxiously.

Suddenly, he understood why Arthur had commanded his presence.

"Arthur plans to attack," Vulcan answered, setting his hammer aside. "He will ride south with the full strength of the Round Table in a campaign against the Survivalists. Queen Isabel, who tended the wounded from Sir Lancelot's mission, strongly opposes him.

"'What can swords and lances do,' she asks, 'against men with guns?'

"'We'll ride them down,' he says. 'Down into the ground.'

"'But guns,' she cries. 'Rogues with rifles.'

"'They've never faced a full army of mounted knights,' he answers.

"And that's surely true," Vulcan added.

"In short," Giraffe said, "the king is determined?"

"Yes," said Vulcan.

He lifted Lancelot's red-hot breastplate from the fire with his tongs and set it on the anvil and began to hammer the other side.

"That's why I'm working day and night to reinforce all the knights' armor and to strengthen their weapons. I wish I had Kumquat to help me."

"Speaking of Kumquat," said Giraffe, "I wonder if you could forge a little something for him?"

"I'd be happy to, Giraffe, if I had time," Vulcan replied between hammer blows. "But, as you can surely see, the king's needs must come first."

"Yes, I understand," Giraffe replied. "But as we've been talking I've had an idea how we can support Arthur's troops and treat Kumquat's allergies both at the same time."

"You're a wizard, Giraffe," Vulcan chuckled as he turned from the anvil to pump his bellows. "But I can't imagine how you can pull off such a fancy trick. After all, nobody, not even Dr. Isabel, knows how to cure Kumquat."

"Think about it, Vulcan. Haven't you already designed a pollen mask for him, you and the queen?"

"Yes, we did," Vulcan admitted as he snatched Lancelot's breastplate and plunged it in a tub of water. "Queen Isabel created a fine screen, and I forged a mask with airtight goggles to fit. But Kumquat never got much use out of it. He couldn't eat since we had to cover his mouth; he couldn't talk so anybody could understand him; and he found it too uncomfortable to sleep in. There it is over on the shelf. Kumquat returned it to me when he left.

"I was sorry to see him go, Giraffe. He was a very nice boy and, as I told his dad, a promising smith; but he couldn't work iron in that mask even though he tried. He couldn't see well enough, especially when smoke covered the goggles."

Vulcan pulled Lancelot's sizzling breastplate out of the tub and shoved it onto a shelf with Gawain's glove and other armor he'd fixed. Then he limped over to his bench for a breather.

"But for encountering the out-of-doors, Vulcan," Giraffe insisted, "for walking or stretching his scales or flying about, your mask provided Kumquat help and comfort, isn't that right?"

"Yes," Vulcan admitted, "except it was a nuisance to

get on and off. Wasn't it, Kumquat?" Vulcan asked the sturdy young dragon who had appeared at the door of the forge.

"I'm not very handy at fastenings," Kumquat answered, holding his head down and away from Vulcan and Giraffe.

"What a courteous young dragon," Giraffe said to himself.

"Is that why you left it here at the forge when you went away?" he asked.

"Yes, Giraffe, it was so much trouble to put on and take off, I decided to do without. I'm alone so much of the time nowadays my sneezing doesn't really matter to anyone but me."

"You should have seen Kumquat trying to adjust the straps of that thing," Vulcan said, laughing and giving his good leg a whack. "I nearly always had to help him make it airtight. And taking it off—well, he twitched his scales and shook his neck and scraped his jaw on the doorpost and threw his head up and down. One night when I'd banked the fire and left the forge early and wasn't able to help him, the poor kid had to go home with that mask still dangling around his neck. Believe me, Giraffe," he said, wiping a speck of soot from his eye, "it was way too much trouble."

"More trouble," Giraffe asked, "than a full suit of armor?"

"A suit of armor?" asked Vulcan.

"A suit of armor?" asked Kumquat, almost breaking into a sneeze.

"A suit of armor!" the smith cried out again and stamped his good foot. "Oh, Giraffe! I believe I'm beginning to understand. You are a wizard.

"Well, young fellow," he said, turning to Kumquat, "Giraffe has found you a new profession—if you are ready for it."

"I'm willing to try anything to earn my way in the kingdom."

"What about the wages of war?" Giraffe proposed. "King Arthur's rule has been threatened, as Vulcan just told me, by the Survivalists, dangerous invaders with buckskin horses and firearms; the king is determined to drive them back into Colorado. Do you have the courage, Kumquat, to rally to your king in this perilous time?"

"Tell me, Giraffe, what I must do to serve his majesty. If he will command me, I will march by his side."

"I am sure, Kumquat, once Vulcan forges the equipment you will need," Giraffe assured the eager recruit, "King Arthur will rely heavily on your support, just as he accepted the victorious assistance of your father's father, Uther Pendragon, long ago in the war to save Britain."

Then turning to Vulcan, he said, "The Round Table has never faced mountain men furnished with firearms; but mountain men have never faced a patriotic, fully fledged dragon. If you transform Kumquat's mask into a helmet, Vulcan, and forge armor for his head and his ears, I believe we can even the sides."

✠ ✠ ✠

When Giraffe crossed the moat and entered Camelot under the castle's virtually real portcullis, he found himself in the midst of turmoil.

Almost all of the knights were assembled in the courtyard; and, with the assistance of squires and dragons, they were donning their armor and testing their weapons. It had been some time since the whole Round Table was mobilized, and there was much to do. Sir Dinadan, whose armor fit no one but himself, had been easily outfitted. King Arthur's armor was plated with gold and his Excalibur, even after several years' neglect, shone in the spring sunlight. Among the other knights, confusion reigned.

"These aren't my greaves," cried Sir Tristram. "They aren't even mates."

"Where is my raven helmet?" shouted Sir Bors. "I can't go into battle bare-headed." He looked around for a minute and exclaimed, "That's it. Gareth, you're wearing my helmet!"

"Not likely,"Sir Gareth replied. "My mother gave me this helmet. Great uncle Lot was wearing it when he was beheaded on the third crusade. He was a victorious warrior."

"I guess you're right," Sir Bors acknowledged on a closer look. "That's not a raven; it's a gull, I see now. But where's my helmet?"

"Here, sir knight," whispered Nectarine. "I buffed it against my scales. See how it shines."

Sir Galahad was completely dressed in his flashy brass gear, of course.

"I think he wears it to bed," Sir Dinadan had once speculated.

But most of the others were at least partially unprotected.

"Has Vulcan finished my breastplate?" Sir Lancelot asked with exasperation. "It's taken less time for my bruise to heal than for him to hammer out that dent."

"Look at my shield," cried Sir Tarquin. "The paint has been chipped off, and my unicorn looks like a donkey!"

This clamor that Arthur's fifty knights made trying to get themselves equipped for battle was intensified by Queen Isabel's complaints.

"No, Arthur, no," she was crying. "You don't understand what men with guns can do. You and your knights won't have a chance. I didn't marry you to become a widow!

"Speak to him, Giraffe," she implored her old friend as he approached her. "He won't listen to me."

"My dear," the king assured her, "those thugs have never faced a line of fully armored warriors, have they, Giraffe?"

"No, your majesty, nor ever seen such a sight, I should believe, although, according to Vulcan, they have encountered a small band of your knights."

"Yes," said the queen, "and sent them scampering home."

"It will be different, Isabel my love, when they face me at the head of the combined Round Table. We will cow them with our arms and our discipline, I promise you, and drive them like chaff before us. We will make them stubble to our swords, won't we, Lancelot?"

"No question, my liege. Once Vulcan repairs my breastplate, I'll be ready to ride."

"And you, Sir Tristram, are you ready?"

"Ready, your majesty, if someone can help me find my other greave."

"We are all eager for battle," said Sir Gawain as he struggled to tug on his gloves. "Look at young Galahad over there!"

And a shout went up from the whole Round Table, except for Sir Kay, who was inside adjusting his helmet.

"We are ready for battle; bring on those Survivalists!"

"But Lancelot," cried the queen as the shout subsided, "you still walk hunched over like an old beggar. And, Gawain, the hand you scraped on a tree while escaping the Survivalists isn't nearly healed. Wait a few days, at least, my king, so you can fight at full strength."

"No, my dear, delay will look like cowardice. We must meet the enemy's challenge, and we must meet it now. If we are brave, we are already half way to victory. Sir Dinadan did not hesitate to enter the monster's flaming mouth, did he, Giraffe?"

"No, your majesty, and he is determined to embrace this new quest. In fact, he has just asked me once again to be his mount. But there may be some merit in the queen's counsel," Giraffe continued. "A battle is always subject to uncertainty, especially a battle organized in haste: remember Camlann. Have you tried diplomacy, your majesty?"

"I have, Giraffe, I am almost ashamed to say. I sent my most gentle and eloquent knight, Sir Kay, to treat with those ruffians, and he was lucky to return alive."

"They stripped his armor and shaved his beard," said Sir Lancelot, hiding a snigger behind his shiny glove, "and they tied him backwards on his horse."

"He made quite a sight galloping up to the castle," added young Galahad.

"It was an insult to Camelot and to me," the king said, giving Galahad and his father a hard look. "It was an intolerable insult. Sir Kay will not even show his face in the courtyard, and rightly, until he has fastened it—hidden it, really—in his helmet. He must be avenged."

"Giraffe," the queen begged her old friend, "can't you think of something to stop this madness? Maybe you could meet with the Survivalists as the king's ambassador?"

"I'm sorry, Isabel," Giraffe responded. "I believe the king has done all he can to persuade the Survivalists to remain on their side of the Colorado border."

"Thank you, Giraffe," said the king. "If your leg is not too painful, I hope you will accompany us in battle."

"I will, your majesty, and, in fact, I have a plan of attack."

"I'm always glad to hear one of your ideas, Giraffe, although I doubt even you can help me much in the conduct of war. However, let's hear it."

"What mount have you chosen?"

"I have decided to ride Trigger."

"Trigger, your majesty?" Giraffe asked with astonishment.

"Yes, Giraffe, Trigger, a western pony for a western campaign."

"Sheriff Cody from South Dakota," Queen Isabel explained, "presented Trigger to the king for a wedding present and 'as a sign of the peace and respect subsisting between our lands'—to use his own words. I have tried to persuade the king to ask the sheriff for assistance in this difficult time. But to no avail."

"My dear wife," the king said with a deep sigh, "this is our fight. The Survivalists have not invaded—not even raided—Cody's county."

"But he's expert with a gun," the queen rejoined, "he and his deputies. He's famous for his sharpshooting."

"True, my dear, we have all witnessed his feats of marksmanship; but this is our fight. And with a mount like Trigger under me I have nothing to fear."

"We will defeat and scatter the Survivalists, my queen," swore Sir Dinadan, "or none of us will return alive."

"That's what I fear, brave knight," wailed the queen. "What difference does it make to me, Giraffe, that Trigger carries my dear husband into this terrible battle?"

"Not Trigger," shouted Peach, who had just flown through the gate. "The saddler says he is foundered in the left front, your majesty."

"Foundered, is he?" the king responded with a growl. "Then who will I ride? Not Champion, he's too old. Not Arianne, she's in foal. Not Frisky or Bucephalus or Old Goat. I need a decent mount. A horse, a horse, my kingdom for a horse."

"I have a suggestion, your majesty," said Giraffe. "Why not present yourself before your enemies astride a dragon, as you did in times past? That should make them cower."

"A dragon?" the king replied with a rising voice. "A dragon, draco. Just like the times when we rode down the Saxons? Yes, yes, Giraffe, a great idea." After a pause, he asked, "What dragon? Charlton has traveled up north to look for work. Persimmon is old; besides, he's a cook. And as for little Peach or Nectarine—even if one of them were able to carry me, the Survivalists would laugh at us."

"What about Kumquat, your majesty?"

"Kumquat?" the king replied with a snort. "The sufferer? Now there's a loose dragon. Charging along in this spring weather, he would be more of a danger to my knights than to the Survivalists. Can't you see him swinging his great head from side to side in a fit of sneezing? He would incinerate us all before we reached the field of battle. No, Giraffe, not Kumquat."

"Not even if he were wearing a pollen-proof helmet, your majesty?"

"A pollen-proof helmet, Giraffe? Tell me about it."

"Queen Isabel—or perhaps I should say Dr. Isabel—which do you prefer?"

"Get on with it, Giraffe. My queen, you say?"

"Yes, your majesty. She developed a pollen filter, a fine screen, and Vulcan has set it in a dragon helmet, made to fit Kumquat. I've taken the liberty of fitting him with one of the old dragon saddles you brought over to Montana from Britain, the very one you rode at Mount Badon, in fact. With a little adjustment, the groom has made it perfectly snug. Kumquat, who is eager to serve Camelot and to be your mount, waits outside with the horses—a little to the side, of course. Are you ready, my lord? We await your command."

The king, followed by the whole Round Table, strode through the portcullis gate, over the drawbridge, and worked his way through his knights' horses until he reached Kumquat. He looked the young dragon in the goggles, confirmed the disposition of his helmet with a jerk, tested his saddle, and, giving his queen a confident look, mounted this fiery steed. He swung his right leg vigorously across the dragon's spine and shook the reins to make sure they were firmly fixed to Kumquat's long scaly neck. Then, giving Giraffe a salute, he summoned his bugler, Roland, who had joined him from France a long time ago.

"Sound march," he commanded as Roland brought his palfrey fairly close to Kumquat's side. "Sound march."

✠ ✠ ✠

The march of Arthur's army south through the woods to meet the Survivalists was accomplished in two stages: one, which took them the entire afternoon, down the southern road from Camelot; the other, which they made at night after a hearty meal and many pledges of bravery, to the field of battle. It was after midnight when Arthur reached the verge of the contested estates.

"I want to take these rogues by surprise if I can," he explained to Giraffe who limped along beside him. "I'll send scouts out ahead of the main army after we make camp. If we can catch them fording a stream, the way I took the Saxons at Glenford and on the banks of the Bassus, we'll destroy them before they can get their pistols out of the holsters."

His memories of ancient victories and his anticipation of another victory made the king laugh out loud and caused Kumquat to prance from side to side—almost knocking Sir Dinadan off Giraffe's back.

The road had led beside the cave of Pineapple and Persimmon, and both of them, along with Mango, who dreamed of the day when she might be big enough to carry Arthur into battle, waved at the knights as they trotted by. They blew billowing flames like flags into the air to encourage the army.

"Kumquat, Kumquat, my son," Persimmon shouted between bursts of patriotic enthusiasm, "fight bravely! Remember Mount Badon!"

As scouts, Arthur selected, not the gaudy Galahad, who volunteered with great bravado, but Sir Tristram, who had been raised in the woods and was famous as a huntsman, the tiny Sir Dinadan, who scouted on foot, of course, and Sir Kay, who had recently practiced hiding from sight. Sir Lancelot proclaimed his special fitness for the chore.

"I'll creep up on them like a fog," Lancelot said with a swagger that made his glittering armor rattle, "and sneak back with the word."

"That Lancelot," Giraffe muttered.

Arthur, after consideration, sent Tristram, Dinadan, and Kay.

An hour after the scouts' departure, the army assembled and trotted off. They traveled as quietly as possible, attempting to minimize the clanking of their armor, the squeaking of their bridles, and the different sounds of their horses, the whinnying, bucking, stomping and jingling of harness bells.

"We might move more secretly," Giraffe thought to himself, "if our armor had been better oiled and if our weapons and shields had not been shined so bright."

As it was, the full moon gleamed and glinted from the column as it clattered along.

"I suppose our knights would feel ashamed," he said under his breath, "to appear in shabby gear."

Sir Galahad's suit seemed almost to sparkle whether the moon glanced on it or not.

"At least," muttered Giraffe as he stumbled along, "the scouts will have no trouble in finding us."

As the light of morning descended from the trees, the scouts returned. They brought bad news.

"The Survivalists must have detected us somehow," Sir Tristram reported to Arthur. "They have taken up their formation on the far side of the meadow yonder, waiting for our attack."

"The horsemen are mounted in a line over there," Sir Dinadan reported. "The riflemen are kneeling in front of them."

"How many are there?" asked King Arthur.

"About forty horsemen riding buckskins, your majesty," Sir Kay estimated. "And eight or ten riflemen."

"A dozen at least," Dinadan insisted. "Great big men all of them."

"Bigger than you, anyway," said King Arthur with a smile.

"Giraffe," the king said in a loud whisper, "you accompany me to the edge of the woods to see this formidable force. The rest remain quietly here under Sir Lancelot's command. Have a little bread and jerky. You too, Galahad: you'll be needing it."

The meadow was lovely in the early morning light.

There were two grassy slopes going down and two gentle rises. "Easy for horses and dragons," Giraffe thought, "if not for old giraffes." On the farther of these slopes, the king and Giraffe discerned their foe.

There were about forty horsemen— "To our fifty," the king murmured—all of them already mounted; and, as Sir Dinadan had reported, a dozen riflemen.

"I should have mobilized my archers," Arthur admitted to Giraffe, "but it's too late now."

The meadow, which presented smooth turf all the way across, was adorned with little clumps of wildflowers, chiefly primroses, daisies and buttercups; but Giraffe also noticed white and blue and deep maroon blossoms everywhere. It reminded him of the meadow he'd shared with Zane and Zack and Ella until a few days ago.

It struck the king differently. "I'm glad Kumquat has that pollen-proof helmet—if it works."

After they had examined the situation for several minutes, the king spoke.

"We must line up over here out of range, and then, when we're in formation, ride against them, ride over them."

"But as we approach, your majesty," Giraffe suggested, "their firearms will take a greater and greater toll."

"True, Giraffe, but we must bring them to the point of our lances."

"Remember, your majesty, the effect of a single bullet on Sir Lancelot's breastplate."

"But Lancelot didn't fall, Giraffe, although, as you may remind me, he is the strongest of my knights. And Vulcan has reinforced all the breastplates since then—and made armor to protect the throats and chests of all our mounts—except, of course, for Kumquat and you, Giraffe."

✠ ✠ ✠

The king mounted Kumquat the moment he and Giraffe had rejoined the army, whose members—especially the young dragon and the tiny knight—had been anxiously awaiting their chief.

"Sound assembly," he commanded Roland.

Almost before the last notes of the bugle call had died away on the fresh spring air, the knights of the Round Table assumed a regular front in the meadow, stationing themselves, knight by knight, just south of the forest in plain sight of the Survivalists. Giraffe with Sir Dinadan astride took the extreme left as King Arthur had commanded; the king, mounted on Kumquat and accompanied by Roland on his palfrey, took the right. Once formed, the army paused so their foes might appreciate the force arrayed against them. Sir Galahad, always greedy for glory, kept thrusting out of formation until his father, who anchored the center of Arthur's line, threatened him with a good spanking and ordered him back. The sun, rising to the left in a cloudless sky, gleamed on the row of armor and glittered on the points of the lances.

The enemy, however, whose bravery lay in their guns and their marksmanship, were not impressed.

"Look at the tin soldiers," they shouted and laughed. "How much hot lead do you figger it will take to knock them all over?"

"You get the big dude with the shiny suit, Amos," said one of the riflemen. "I'll plug the stout hombre in gold over on the left."

"Let me put a bullet in him, Obediah," cried another, "or, at least, in the funny-looking pony he's riding. Look at the blinkers that critter is wearing—and where did he get that scalloped mane?"

"No matter, Jonah," shouted a yellow-bearded horseman. "Once you or Micah get him in your sights, I allow as how he'll go down just like all the rest."

"I'm going to drop that big, scrawny critter with all the spots on the other end," another of the riflemen cried out.

"Don't waste a bullet on him, Nahum," Yellow Beard shouted. "It looks like he'll fall down by himself; besides, he doesn't even have a rider."

"I'd still like to take him," Nahum muttered.

The rude Saxons arrayed across from Arthur's knights, except for their weapons, were quite like the enemies they had conquered long ago in the borders of England and Scotland. The knights were not afraid.

"Sound charge, Roland!" the king commanded with a roar; and as the bugle echoed across the meadow, the knights, almost as a single being, roused their mounts and moved at a steady trot down the first flowery slope.

The riflemen across the meadow held their fire until Arthur's front rose above the crest of the first rise; and then, at the order of Yellow Beard, they loosed a volley. Twelve shots rang out across the meadow and eight of Arthur's knights fell back; two, three, four of them gradually tipped off their mounts. A couple of horses went down.

A bullet hit Sir Lancelot on his breastplate.

"Exactly where they got me before," he cried out in anger.

But he kept his seat, and, after staggering briefly, he and his horse charged on.

One bullet knocked the gull from Sir Gareth's helmet; another tore off one of Sir Tristram's greaves and wounded his calf. But like Lancelot, he continued to ride. Another bullet, as Arthur saw while he himself maintained the charge, got Tarquin in the donkey.

More knights fell in the valley after another burst of riflefire, and several, who had been staggered by the barrage, dropped back out of line.

Arthur reined Kumquat to a stop and surveyed the field. Ten or fifteen of his men were struggling to stay mounted on runaway horses; as many more lay here and there around the meadow, flailing their arms and legs like turtles. Sir Dinadan was among them because Giraffe, as he started down the second slope, had stepped with his bad leg into a gopher hole and gone down very hard, tossing Sir Dinadan as he fell.

The Survivalists, Arthur saw, confidently held their formation. The riflemen, still in the kneeling position, were loading for another volley; and the horsemen, prancing and cavorting impatiently behind them, had not yet taken their pistols from the holsters.

"We must withdraw," Arthur recognized with helpless anger.

"Roland, Roland!" he shouted.

But before he could give an order to his bugler, a

hail of bullets stopped him. One pinged Excalibur, almost knocking that invulnerable blade from his hand; another ricocheted off his arm, causing him to lose control of Kumquat's reins. Kumquat was hit, too. One bullet tore into the dragon's scaly neck; another one, worse still, ripped his helmet away from his face.

"We must withdraw!"

"No, my liege," cried the dragon, his voice very clear now that the pollen-proof helmet had been breached. "Hang on tight," he said, and he thrust his nose into the flowers of the meadow.

He drew two, three, four deep breaths into his lungs. Then he spread his wings, which were almost as great as his brother, Charlton's, and took flight.

Giraffe, who was fixed in place on the other side of the meadow, with his legs crumpled under him, saw Kumquat take off. He feared at first, as he watched King Arthur borne into the sky, that the young dragon, who was soaring away from the line of battle, had fled and carried his leader to an ignominious retreat.

But once Kumquat reached a certain height, as Giraffe traced his progress, the dragon lowered his great left wing, circled back until he flanked the Survivalist line, and swooped. Almost before Giraffe realized the pollen-proof helmet had fallen from Kumquat's face and was dangling from his neck, the dragon bore down on the Survivalists, spouting flame in great red-orange bursts from his gaping mouth and his hideously flared nostrils. This sight frightened Giraffe although he was safely out of the line of fire; the Survivalists, as they watched the dragon bearing down on them, seemed petrified. But only for a second: in his first pass, sneezing burst after burst, Kumquat incinerated several men, roasted more, and shattered the resolve of the rest. As he soared off to draw fresh pollen for another attack, his great tail swatted the only Survivalist brave enough to resist, Yellow Beard, and knocked him from his mount.

When Kumquat landed in a patch of daisies to re-load, Arthur, who had hardly recovered his breath, found the strength to cry out, "Enough, Kumquat, we have routed them. The victory is ours. Enough. The knights will chase all that are left back across the border. You have destroyed them, my fine fellow. They will never trouble Camelot again."

Arthur was right. The Round Table had won the battle. Several knights, among them Sir Tristram, despite his wounded calf, Sir Kay, who had finally raised his beaver, and Sir Lancelot with his dented breastplate, had ridden into the woods, pursuing the panic-striken Survivalists. But not Galahad, poor Galahad. His horse had been shot from under him, and he was strutting angrily about the meadow, waving his sword and cursing his luck.

"Dad and Sir Tristram are having all the fun, cutting down those scared Survivalists and grabbing the loot."

Other knights were less lucky than Galahad. Arthur counted eleven men lying wounded and two or three others wandering dazedly around the meadow.

"I've lost my horse, Rowdy," Sir Bors complained to the king. "When the Survivalists' shot knocked me off, Rowdy took fright and ran away. I don't know where. I hope he's not hurt."

Sir Tarquin looked among the wildflowers for pieces of his shield.

"My father, King Bagdemagus, gave me that shield," he told Arthur, "and made me vow to keep it forever."

Among the supine warriors, who had suffered a variety of wounds and bruises, were Sir Gareth, the gallant, whose helmet a Survivalist bullet had driven into his left eye; Sir Ector, the unfortunate, whose horse had broken down at almost his first step and tossed the knight on his head; Sir Perimedes, the saracen, brother of Sir Palomides, whose left arm was smashed—he didn't remember how—and swung limply from his shoulder; Sir Bedevere, the old—much too old, as Arthur had told him, for this action—who had tumbled from his horse when it shied at the first volley and who was hardly able to move; the youthful Sir Parsifal, who had sustained a shot in the back; and, of course, Sir Dinadan.

All of them were disoriented, not aware of who had won the battle until Arthur told them, and, in some cases, not even then. Giraffe was also unable to rise although fully aware of the course of the battle and conscious of the victory.

"Sir Galahad," said King Arthur, who dismounted to survey the field, "you seem to be sound; assist Giraffe and, if he's able to walk, help Sir Dinadan to support him back to Camelot.

"Sir Tarquin," he continued, "your task is to lead Sir Gareth until you can release him to the queen, that is, to Dr. Isabel.

"Sir Bors, I trust you to attend Sir Bedevere, who

may not quite know where he is. Don't leave him until you've settled him safe at home.

"I will lead Kumquat, who has the most terrible wound; and we will take the front in case he has a need to sneeze. Roland, my lad, sound retreat; then ride ahead as fast as that palfrey will carry you and deliver to Queen Isabel the news of our victory."

As the king was organizing this triumphal march back home to Camelot, those knights who had pursued their beaten foes into the woods returned to the meadow.

"We have totally dispersed the Survivalists, your majesty," Sir Lancelot reported.

"One of them, Yellow Beard, who seemed to be their leader," Sir Tristram said, "scrambled up into a birch tree, and when I thrust my lance against it, he fell. But he sneaked away on all fours, and I let him go."

"The rest, my liege," Sir Lancelot crowed, "vanished without pausing to challenge me to a single pass at arms."

"It will be hot day in January," said Sir Kay, "before they show their faces to us again."

"What loot?" cried Sir Galahad.

There wasn't much: no bags of gold and jewels dropped in panic; no encrusted shields discarded in flight; no magic helmets wrested from the necks or cut away with the heads of royal foes; no famous swords purchased at a coward's life; only a half-dozen old bandoliers partially empty of bullets, three pistols, four sooty rifles, a singed shirt sleeve, a couple of steaming cowboy hats, and an odd boot.

"I took that black hat off Yellow Beard," boasted

Sir Tristram, "or, rather, off the ground where he dropped it when he skittered off into the bracken."

This hat Sir Tristram was allowed to keep as a trophy; the other traces of their beaten foe Arthur's army left behind to litter the meadow in which their great victory was won.

✠ ✠ ✠

"They've been beaten, destroyed," Queen Isabel cried out as she saw Roland race up to the castle.

She descended from the main turret, at the window of which she had watched and listened all day.

"I knew how it would be," she said to herself as she hurried down the genuine imitation marble staircase.

"Oh," she whispered, as if she were afraid of being overheard, "if only my king has survived!"

"Queen Isabel, Queen Isabel," the bugler shouted as he reined his palfrey before the raised drawbridge. "I bring news!"

"Is the king alive? Quickly, fellow, is the king alive?"

"Yes, my queen, alive and victorious. We have driven the Survivalists from Montana."

"Is he hurt, Roland?"

"Slightly, my queen."

"How slightly? Tell me, man!"

"A bullet struck his left arm, your majesty, and seems to have paralyzed it. Luckily, his armor deflected the shot, so he was not wounded. He is leading Kumquat home. The dragon has been hit in the neck."

"And others?" asked Dr. Isabel.

She had called Dr. Oscar the orangutan before the army departed, and he had arrived at Camelot with supplies on the first train. Gloria the gorilla accompanied him and brought several flasks of her banana punch.

"It both calms and exhilarates," she assured Dr. Isabel.

Several raccoons, all of them handy in chiropractic medicine, came, too. Among them was her old friend Rudolph, who was also the father of her chief assistant, Katie.

"Thank you for joining Katie and me, Rudolph. We need help."

"The point, Queen Isabel, is that you need *my* help."

So the queen was ready to treat all the casualties the battle had produced. She had furnished the banquet hall as an annex to her clinic, ordering the castle staff to remove the Round Table and replace it with circles of beds. She had summoned Vulcan, certain even before Roland told her about Sir Gareth's wound, the smith would have to help her nurses remove the knights' armor. And when she learned about Giraffe's damaged leg, she ordered the castle staff to erect an adjustable sling in the courtyard so he could be treated and sustained.

"And Katie, don't forget the asbestos suits," she said. "We'll need those."

Dr. Isabel was ready.

It was a good thing.

The army, which reached Camelot late in the afternoon, bore little resemblance to the spirited troop that had galloped off to battle only the day before. The armor of several knights, besides Sir Gareth's and Sir Tristram's, dripped with blood. Some of the returning mounts were bleeding and some were lame. Quite a lot of armor, besides Sir Lancelot's and King Arthur's, was dented; and all of it showed stains. Even the stain-proof suit of Sir Galahad looked a little the worse for wear. Other knights carried only broken lances or damaged shields.

Sir Lancelot, Sir Dinadan, and even Sir Gareth, who was blinded with pain, tried to muffle their moans; but a doleful murmur accompanied the victorious army's progress. Those knights who returned on foot attempted, as they approached Camelot, to limp as little as possible or at least to limp with spirit. King Arthur, who trudged in front leading Kumquat, although clearly exhausted, stood tall before the queen and projected a triumphant demeanor. His left arm dangled at his side.

"We have won a great victory, my queen," Arthur announced to Isabel, who fought back tears. "Have we not, my brave knights?"

A strangled, intermittent shout confirmed this royal plea.

"But now, madam doctor, we all need your kind attention—and especially the heroic Kumquat, who has suffered a most serious wound."

As attendants surrounded the dragon, who was bleeding profusely, the king said further, "The bullet seems to have lodged in his throat, doctor; I hope you can remove it."

The king collapsed and nearly fainted, and Dr. Isabel's staff swept into action.

Dr. Oscar, Gloria, Rudolph, Vulcan, Katie, and Dr. Isabel had each one spent a moment considering the wretched state of the army and then, without hesitation, they set about the tasks of healing that confronted them. Vulcan, aided by Peach and Nectarine, undressed the knights as the castle staff settled them in bed. Dr. Oscar concerned himself chiefly with bandaging wounds, a skill for which he was famous all over Montana, while Rudolph and Katie worked with bones and bruises, starting, of course, with the king's elbow. Dr. Isabel did the surgery, first addressing Kumquat's neck wound and then, once Vulcan had removed his helmet, Sir Gareth's ruined eye. Gloria the gorilla passed almost invisibly among the fallen warriors, dispensing calm or exhilaration as it was needed.

Late at night when the work was done, Dr. Isabel stumbled, exhausted, into the castle courtyard to visit Giraffe. He was awake and, considering the labor and the pain he had endured, in good spirits.

"Is your sling comfortable, Giraffe? Does it provide you enough support?"

"It works fine, doctor; if I need to take more weight off my leg, I just wrap my tongue around this wheel and give it a turn."

"How is your pain? Did Katie wrap your leg tight enough?"

"Actually, your majesty, Rudolph did the job, and he handled it quite professionally, as he himself said. He found no broken bone so I should be walking on my own in a day or two."

"A day or two! I want you to remain in that sling for

a full week—until I release you. Sir Dinadan, who sustained a broken ankle, by the way, has told me how far you fell."

"Very well, doctor. But tell me, how are the others?"

"There were many bad cases. Sir Lancelot received a broken breastbone this time; and Sir Gawain, who should not have tried to hold a sword—as I told him—has hurt his hand very badly. I may have to amputate his little finger—serve him right. Sir Tristram's achilles tendon was severed, and, although I did my best, I'm uncertain whether he will walk or ride again. But I'm most worried about Sir Gareth. His eye is gone. Once the socket has healed, I'll insert a glass eye, that is, if his brain isn't affected.

"There are other wounds as well and many broken bones, especially broken legs and ankles; and a few nasty dislocations. The king will have to wear a sling, although not as big a one as yours, Giraffe, for several weeks."

"What about Kumquat?"

"I was able to save his life, but his wound is really terrible. I hardly know how to tell you this, but I had to cut out his fire glands, all of them. The bullet that hit him splattered them, Giraffe, and I couldn't remove it safely without taking them, too. Kumquat will survive, but he'll never again spout dragon fire—not even a puff of smoke. His glands were packed with pollen, so he may not ever suffer hay fever anymore; but, whether he does or not, nobody needs to fear his sneezes. Maybe that will be one good thing to come out of this awful victory of ours.

"It was a victory, wasn't it, Giraffe?" the queen asked her friend. "As great a victory as we could have hoped for?"

"Yes, your majesty."

“We must not forget, Giraffe,” said the queen.

✠ ✠ ✠

King Arthur’s castle, once the Round Table was waxed and buffed and restored to its place in the banquet hall, prepared for a great ceremony, the creation, not only of a new knight, but of a new knight of the Round Table.

Flags flew from every turret of the castle; the walls, inside and out, were shined. Painters re-marbled the stones of the courtyard, at one end of which, carpenters erected a dais. It was mounted by two thrones, both made, as the queen directed, of solid mahogany. At the other end, they constructed a platform for Roland from the remains of Giraffe’s sling. The drawbridge was lowered and the portcullis raised.

King Arthur and Queen Isabel, dressed in royal purple and adorned with their freshly polished crowns, as the occasion required, sat enthroned on the dais; Kumquat and Giraffe stood, one on either side of Roland’s platform, facing them. Kumquat, poised at attention, wore his helmet, no longer enclosed with screen, and a fine chestplate—not quite big enough, however, to hide his beautiful new bandage. Giraffe, although his damaged leg was wrapped almost to the hip—and that took some wrapping—stood quite erect. Lined along the walls of the courtyard on either side stood the king’s knights, their armor shined just for today. All of them, some with the aid of canes and crutches, remained stiffly upright except for Sir

Tristram and Sir Gareth, each of whom, fully armed, had been pushed into place in a wheelchair. A purple satin sling fastened with the replica of a fine penannular broach supported the king's left arm.

In the plastic balconies above, overlooking this splendid scene, crowded the citizens of Camelot, both dragon and human folk, and many other people, among them raccoons and apes, who attended as honored guests.

"Look at our boy, Persimmon," exclaimed Pineapple, who was one of the onlookers. "Isn't he grand in his helmet and plate—and bandage?"

"Yes, he is a credit to us; but no tears now, my love, please, no tears!"

At a nod from the king, Roland raised his bugle and sounded the call to advance. As the notes echoed around the walls, Kumquat crept with dignity through the attentive lines of knights and stopped with a bow and a respectful, but smokeless, salute before the royal pair.

Arthur rose and, after a little difficulty with his robe, produced Excalibur. He stepped to the edge of the dais and proclaimed, "Crouch, Kumquat, and receive from a grateful sovereign the proper reward of loyalty and valor."

After the hero took his stance, the king continued.

"I dub you Sir Kumquat and welcome you into the society of the Round Table. Rise, Sir Kumquat, and greet your new friends."

So began the suffering dragon's long and honorable career as Arthur's thane. From that time on, he labored every day at the forge with Vulcan, who rejoiced in such a talented and cool-headed assistant; and at night he attended the king, crouching at the Round Table in his designated place, and shared in the stories of his fellow knights, stories, as the years passed, that wove them all, more than anything else, into one heroic company.

✠ ✠ ✠

A few hours after the ceremony that marked the beginning of Kumquat's advancement, a few hours after the cheers, after the embraces of family and friends, after the banquet of celebration with its boasts and pledges, Queen Isabel accompanied Giraffe to the Camelot crossroads or, rather, the Camelot crosstracks.

"You should remain with us a little longer," the queen insisted. "At least until I can replace the wrapping on your hip and make sure you are fit to travel."

"I am fit enough, my queen. This wrapping that Dr. Oscar the orangutan has contrived allows me to walk quite well. It reminds me of the bandage he created for the tail of Billy the beaver. Do you remember that?"

"Of course, Giraffe, but Billy didn't have to walk on his tail."

"True, your majesty, but I'm moving along pretty comfortably, all the same. And I feel an urge to wander."

"I will miss you, Giraffe, and you're not even wearing the phone I gave you for Christmas so I can call when I need you."

"You are always in my heart, Queen Isabel; I hope I will always be in yours."

"Always, Giraffe."

"Then we will always be able to consult one another—much better than we could by phone."

"Yes," she said and bit her lip.

"Please give my love to Fergus and Isabella when you call them and, of course, to your dear husband. I will carry you all in my heart."

Then Giraffe turned and headed east.

The last Queen Isabel saw of him, he was walking with a slight limp down the trail that led through Montana woods to the badlands of Dakota and then into Iowa and then, beyond that, to Illinois, Indiana, Ohio and Kentucky.

Departure

✠ ✠ ✠

"There are a couple of dragons at the door, your majesty," Oscar the footman reported one morning to Queen Isabella.

"They must have become lost on the trail to Camelot, Oscar. Will you go out and show them the way? On second thought, maybe you should go, Fergus, my love. You give such clear directions."

Before King Fergus could rise from the breakfast table, however, his father said, "They are not lost, my queen, and they explicitly asked to see you. One of them, who says his name is Charlton, claims to have a letter of introduction. Shall I turn them away?"

"No, Dad," said Fergus, "I believe we should see them, don't you, dear?"

"Very well," Isabella agreed. "After I've finished my coffee."

"Charlton," said Fergus thoughtfully while his wife stirred a second spoonful of sugar into her cup. "Isn't that the dragon whose infected tooth made him attack Arthur and Isabel at Camelot, the dragon Giraffe had to heal?"

"Yes, darling, but I don't know what he could want with us," the queen replied as she sipped her coffee. "I suspect, however, Giraffe is behind it, somehow."

She was quite right. The first thing Charlton the dragon did when he and his bride, Cauliflower, were admitted into the presence of Fergus and Isabella was to present them "This letter of introduction from my great friend and patron, Giraffe."

As she took the letter, Queen Isabella examined her two guests. They made a very good-looking couple. Charlton, who had a fine, iridescent chest, was courtly, and Cauliflower, although she had some trouble keeping her wings furled, had a very pretty profile. And the two of them were very much in love, a fact of the queen's observation that strongly influenced her in their favor.

"Giraffe recommends you as a replacement for our retiring cook, Catherine," the queen said, as she glanced over the letter. "He especially praises your goat cheese soufflé, Charlton. When did he have a chance to sample it?"

"Giraffe visited my family for a few days, your majesty, after he and Sir Dinadan extracted my infected molar; and my dad and I were able to wine and dine him several times."

"Your father is Persimmon, the chief cook at Camelot, I believe," said the king.

"Yes, your majesty, he has prepared King Arthur's food for many years."

"I remember," Queen Isabella said, "enjoying an especially delicious filet mignon when we visited Camelot for Beltane last spring. Did your father roast that?"

"Yes, my queen. Steak is one of his specialties."

"And what are your specialties?"

"I pride myself, chiefly," Charlton replied, "on my poultry and soups. My father, with whom I studied for many years, has said my gravy is better than his."

"This is your wife—Cauliflower, is it?—a very pretty name. Does she plan to assist you?"

"Yes, your majesty, but she specializes in casseroles and salads. And these are quite wonderful, as I believe you will agree," he said as he extended his wings with pride, "that is, if you decide to give us the chance to serve you. Cauliflower is herself a Vegetable, or she was until she consented to take my name."

"Charlton and Cauliflower Fruit?" said the queen, trying over the dragons' names. "If King Fergus and I appoint you our cooks," she asked, "where will you live?"

"Giraffe offered us his cave," Charlton replied, "on the condition you and the king approve."

"His cave?" Isabella exclaimed. "But that is his own home in the middle of Montana. Rudolph and Peter installed the fireplace for him—to help him adjust to our winter weather; and the beavers laid down his moss."

"Yes, my dear," Fergus added with a smile, "and Gloria kept a fresh stalk of bananas always hanging up in a convenient crevice—in case Giraffe ever wanted one."

"There is a stalk hanging there now," said Charlton, "as Giraffe told Cauliflower and me there would be. I do love bananas," he said, and he stretched his left wing self-consciously over his mouth.

"Giraffe invited Charlton to help himself," Cauliflower said, "and I must say he has."

"You've been to Giraffe's cave?" asked the queen.

"Yes, your majesty," replied Charlton. "Giraffe suggested we should drop in on our way here."

"It would be too small for a family," said Cauliflower, "once Charlton and I have started one, but it's fine," she said, pulling her wings tight about her, "for the two of us."

"Yes," said Charlton enthusiastically, "It's a very comfortable cave. We don't need the fireplace. Two can sleep more warmly than one. And, although we're used to rugs, the moss is very soft and quite fire-proof."

"Once we fold our wings," Cauliflower added, "we fit in the cave like matches in a match box."

Before Queen Isabella could respond, King Fergus spoke. "Why don't the two of you stay there then until the queen and I have spoken to Catherine the cook about her plans and decided on your appointment? Return here to the palace, say, on Tuesday morning? Meanwhile, you might visit Allison the alligator and Casper the crocodile, who bask beside the pond just a few steps north of Giraffe's cave, and, perhaps, the raccoons, who dwell nearby. Won't that be a good idea, my queen?"

"Yes, Fergus my love," Isabella answered, although she seemed somewhat distracted, "that seems appropriate under the circumstances.

"But I would like to keep Giraffe's letter," she added, turning to the dragons, "if that's all right with you."

"Of course, your majesty," Charlton responded. "We will attend you and King Fergus on Tuesday, as he has commanded."

✠ ✠ ✠

"What does this mean, my love?" asked Isabella with some alarm as soon as Cauliflower and Charlton had bowed and taken their leave. "Where does Giraffe plan to live if he gives his cave to these dragons?"

"I'm not sure, my dear," Fergus replied, "but he may not plan to live in his cave any longer. It seems that way."

"Not live in his cave; not live near us? What makes you say such a thing?"

"The last time he visited the palace, before he took the train to Camelot, I felt as if you and I were facing a loss, as if Giraffe were leaving us and he knew it. Do you remember how he said goodbye?"

"He told us to take care of one another—and not to forget him.

"'As if we ever could, Giraffe,' I answered and laughed. 'You make it sound like you're not coming back.'"

"Yes, my love, he did. He seemed to be saying goodbye to us for good and all.

"As Giraffe and I walked to the door of the palace," Fergus recollected, "I asked him about this, and he replied in a funny way. He talked about wandering around for a while.

"'Wandering, Giraffe?' I said with a laugh. 'With that game leg, you will be lucky if you are able to wander back to your cave.'

"'Well,' he replied and smiled at me, 'maybe I'll pay a visit to Dr. Oscar and get my hip wrapped. Then I'll be able to do some wandering.'"

"We must call Isabel," Isabella exclaimed, "and find out what she knows."

✠ ✠ ✠

"Isabel darling, it's your sister. I'm calling to find out what you know about Giraffe. He's vanished. Not only that, but he has given his home to a couple of dragons—or so a letter he wrote for them seems to say. Do you or Arthur know about this?"

"Yes, dear, he was here in Camelot a few weeks ago. He supported the king in our struggle against the

Survivalists and participated in our victory. Actually, he fell in the battle."

"Giraffe fell?"

"Yes, Isabella, he stepped in a gopher hole and took a very hard fall."

"But is he okay?"

"I think so. He was quite hearty last week and moving around pretty easily. He sported a wrapping on his left hind leg—the handiwork of Dr. Oscar. He was limping a little—but not much—when we parted at the Camelot crosstracks about ten days ago."

"Then why isn't he back home?" asked Queen Isabella. "Montana is a big state, sister, but he should have returned to the middle—bad leg and all—by now."

"But he wasn't headed home, Isabella. He went east toward Dakota."

"East? I don't understand. What was he thinking?"

"I'm not sure, darling, but he said he was in a mood to wander."

"That's just what he said to Fergus when he left us for Camelot. I'm so worried, Isabel. Do you think he's leaving us?"

"I don't know, but he did make a point of sending you and Fergus his love.

"'Tell them,' he said, 'they will always be in my heart.'"

"Always in his heart? Oh, Giraffe. What did he mean, Isabel? He was leaving us, wasn't he? He was leaving Montana."

"I'm afraid so. That was the impression I got."

"What will we do without Giraffe, Isabel?"

"We must do the best we can; that's what Giraffe would want, don't you agree?"

"Yes," Queen Isabella replied. "That's what he would want. But have you heard anything from him since he left you? I'm so worried."

"Actually," Isabel responded, "I got a call yesterday from the state university in Ames, Iowa that may have come from Giraffe. I couldn't be sure. The connection was so bad. Whoever it was referred me to a book on the domestic diseases of dragons, a subject very interesting to me, as Giraffe would know."

"But do you think it was Giraffe?"

"I couldn't tell. The caller hung up without identifying himself—that's not really like Giraffe, is it? But I've sent off to the University of Chicago for that book. By the way, Isabella, do you and Fergus plan to hire the dragons Giraffe recommended to you?"

"I don't know. I'm so upset I can hardly think about anybody but Giraffe.

"Fergus," she said, putting her hand over the telephone's mouthpiece, "should we hire Charlton and Cauliflower?

"He says 'yes,' we should at least give them a try," she said, taking her hand off the mouthpiece. "Catherine the cook plans to retire and move to Billings. And since Oscar the footman plans to live with her there—another shock for Fergus and me—we also need someone to answer the door. Do you have a suggestion?"

"I do, in fact," Isabel responded. "Charlton's little sister, Mango. She's a very sweet, accommodating dragon, just beginning to fly, I believe. King Arthur and I are served by cousins of hers, who virtually run our castle; and they are very reliable. You commented last spring on the cookery of Persimmon, Mango's father, didn't you, Isabella? And you probably remember Peach and Nectarine as well. They served at table, answered the door, and took care of all the linen. I'm sure Mango, with a little training of course, would do as good a job for you—a much better job than Marian the maid did for Mother."

And so Mango the maid came to the palace of Fergus and Isabella along with Charlton and Cauliflower the cooks; and from that time on, dragons participated in the life of the middle of Montana.

But what about Giraffe?

✠ ✠ ✠

There were signs he had not forgotten—not simply forgotten—his many friends. In addition to Queen Isabel's mysterious phone call, there was the postcard that came for Rudolph the raccoon. It had got soaked and smudged in a rainstorm, which struck Roo's plane when he was bringing the mail over from Camelot; but it seemed to depict a giraffe standing beside Mary Todd Lincoln's home in Lexington, Kentucky.

"Does the giraffe have a bandage on his left hind leg?" Queen Isabella asked Rudolph when he called her at the palace to report this trace of their friend. "What is the return address?"

"The picture is so smudged, your majesty," said Rudolph as he studied it, "I can't say for sure.

"Do you think the giraffe is wearing a bandage?" he asked his wife. "The queen wants to know.

"I believe I see one," he reported, "but Ruth says 'no.' There's no return address. Would you like me to bring the card to the palace so you and the king can examine it?"

Queen Isabella very much wanted to have it. In fact, she was taking stock of all the traces of Giraffe that emerged anywhere in Montana. And there were several. Fred the fox delivered an automatic dust pan simply inscribed "Bo Bo," along with a year's supply of plastic bags, at the mailbox below the dam. Kanga found a recipe for bourbon-flavored mead pinned to her door-hanging one day when she and Roo returned from a visit to the lions; and Gloria the gorilla came across another recipe—for banana julep—stuck to the bottom of one of her flasks.

A subscription for University of North Carolina Medical Journal began without any notice being delivered to Dr. Oscar the orangutan. And one morning as he climbed out of the pond, chewing meditatively on a tangle of green slime, Hal the hippo almost stepped on a beautiful set of Christmas lights. The lights represented all sorts of animals: zebras, lions, possums, moles, and a splendid giraffe, a mate to the one the Isabels had brought back years before from Billings. Neither Allison nor Casper, whom Queen Isabella questioned closely, had any notion how the lights got beside the pond.

"I wonder," Casper snapped, as he was leaving the palace, "why there's no crocodile or alligator."

Queen Isabella herself received from the Billings Bijou a video of *The Wizard of Oz*.

None of these gifts could be explained.

On the morning she opened the package that held this video, Queen Isabella called her sister again.

"Any news of Giraffe, darling?"

"Yes," Queen Isabel responded, "I think so. A pair of ruby slippers has arrived for me from the MGM Studio in Orlando, Florida, or so it says on the box. And I just love them. I always envied you those you bought at Billings, do you remember?"

"Yes, dear, but I never knew you fancied them."

"Any news," asked Queen Isabel, "from the middle of Montana?"

"Yes, sister, nearly every person here has received a gift of some kind: a dustpan, a shovel, a recipe, a box of candied grubs, a subscription, a set of lights for Christmas. Fred the fox has reported to Fergus and me that Casper and Allison have been sent—all the way from Miami Beach—a little awning for their patio. The card says 'Protection against the Montana sun.' But it doesn't say who sent it."

"It's all so mysterious!" said Queen Isabel. "Arthur has received a strange call from Colorado, from Yellow Beard, the leader of the Survivalists we drove back across the border shortly before Giraffe left us."

"I thought you had seen and heard the last of those awful people," Queen Isabella replied. "Are they threatening a new attack? I know Kumquat can't be much help to you anymore, but we could send you our Charlton, if you need him."

"No, Isabella, Yellow Beard is not threatening us at

all. In fact, he's complaining we may be threatening him. The king taught him his lesson."

"What is his complaint?"

"It seems, as he told the king, some of his men have seen a tall, spotted creature browsing the tops of their trees. But when they draw their six-shooters and ride over to investigate, or so Yellow Beard says, the creature has vanished.

"'He seems to fade away,' they report; and when they've reached the place where he stood, they say they can't find a trace. The trees they swear they saw him browsing are quite undisturbed. According to their fearless leader, they are all pretty scared. The king, who naturally assures Yellow Beard of his own mystification, has sent Sir Dinadan on Trigger Jr. to discuss the matter and calm those cowardly cowboys. But it is strange, isn't it?"

✠ ✠ ✠

"Let's ask Rudolf the red-nosed reindeer," King Fergus suggested to his queen one day during a discussion of all these mysterious events, "if he and his partners, Dasher and Dancer and Prancer and Vixen and Comet and Cupid and Donder and Blitzen, have the leisure to help us search for our friend."

"That's a splendid idea, my love," the queen responded, "and late spring should be a very slack time for them—if Santa will agree."

"They know the whole world," said Fergus, "and should be able to scan it in a day or two. If Giraffe is to be found, surely they will find him."

Luckily the reindeer were available, as Isabella had supposed; and after Santa had fastened a personalized pouch full of oats and candy canes around the neck of every one, they set off.

They spread out, each pair selecting a continent or two, and with their eyes peeled for any sign of Giraffe, soared away on their chosen routes. Rudolf searched Africa, especially scanning the Serengeti Plain, Giraffe's childhood home. Dasher and Dancer focused on North America and paid special attention to the track that led from Camelot through Kentucky and across the mountains to Georgia. Two others, Donder and Blitzen—the hardiest of the eight—surveyed Antarctica. Santa's reindeer covered the globe, in short, like Sherwin Williams™ paint used to do. But no Giraffe.

"I'm sorry, my dear Isabella," Santa reported by phone after the search was completed, "but Rudolf reports they found only one tiny trace—a few treetops that had been browsed along the Appalachian Trail between Tennessee and Carolina; and a close examination of the area turned up nothing but a tuft of spotted hair that was caught on a blackberry bramble or the branch of a dogwood tree. Please let us know if you have better luck—Rudolf, of course, is very concerned; and tell us any way we can help you in the search."

"Thank you, Santa," the queen replied. "We are not giving up."

"A funny thing," said Santa before he hung up the phone. "Mrs. Claus, who chiefly collects and studies the mail, has told me she has noticed a remarkable rise in requests for our Giraffe Cuddlies, not in the U. S. A., but in Mexico, Canada, France, Germany, and throughout the middle east."

✠ ✠ ✠

There were a few more signs of their departed friend that, as the months passed, drifted back to Fergus and Isabella in the middle of Montana. Several people to the west of Missoula reported strange sightings, mostly in the night sky. One fellow swore when he and his wife were driving home from a Derby party they saw the stars of the big dipper re-arranged to form the figure of a giraffe—or maybe a horse, his wife suggested. Another told friends how a giraffe had got a leg caught in the chimney of his hunting cabin—a leg with a wrapping on it; and still another reported to the police he had caught a lame giraffe in the headlights of his pickup one night when he was driving home from his beer-and-bowling club—and swerved into the ditch to miss it.

A Boy Scout master complained to his scouts' parents that he couldn't convince his troop that the tall, spotted creature they sighted cropping the tops of trees at dusk on the second day of their camping trip below Grand Teton was a bear. And a little girl assured her parents her pet kitten, Brittney, had been rescued from the roof of the family garage by a tall friendly animal with a prehensile tongue.

Mr. Masters the manager of the Grand Hotel in Billings and Mr. Masters the manager of the Florida Zoo both called King Fergus and Queen Isabella one day to inquire about a telegraph message they had received, the same message in each case. "Kindest memories and regards from your old acquaintance. Giraffe."

"My dear," said King Fergus when he hung up the phone after the second of these calls, "I believe we should assemble all our citizens down at the hall, and canvas these clues of our departed friend. Perhaps, if we gather and study them—all of us together—we may discover his whereabouts or, at any rate, his intentions."

"That's an excellent idea," responded the queen with a smile. "In point of fact, I had the same notion myself. And I hope you won't mind, my dear, but I have already put the wheels in motion. I have directed the foxes to deliver an engraved invitation to each of our citizens to attend us at Friendship Hall this Friday afternoon at three o'clock, and I have sent Charlton and Cauliflower flying to make sure everyone got the message."

"That's fine, Isabella, my love, three o'clock Friday, you say. I'm sure I can re-schedule my dental appointment with Ruth the raccoon for some other time."

✠ ✠ ✠

Friendship Hall, to which Queen Isabella summoned the citizens, had been augmented since Giraffe and his fellow Montanans first carried out the ambitious architectural plans of Rudolph the raccoon. On the far side of Friendship Airfield, which Ella and Hal had stomped level, stood the hangers for the planes of the Montana Air Service and its maintainence buildings. Next to the hall itself, an air terminal had been constructed and then enlarged to house the Montana Postal Service. It had recently been connected to the hall by an enclosed cloister, the transparent glass walls of which preserved the hall's magificent silhouette.

As she surveyed this great facility, the queen entertained many memories and, chiefly, the memory of Giraffe dispatching Roo in *The Fly* on what had proven to be the first rescue mission of the Montana Air Force.

"Oh, Fergus," she cried, "this is all the work of Giraffe."

"Yes," her husband responded, "but, as you know, my love, he would insist on sharing the credit—or in attributing it all to the power of friendship."

"Yes, Fergus," she replied, "yes. Oh, I miss him so much."

As the royal couple, accompanied by Mango, entered, they heard an intense buzz—neighs, snorts, growls, squeaks, purrs, trumpeting—all of it delivered in a tone of worry and anticipation.

"Not in the Florida Zoo, I hope," muttered Ella the elephant. "That pen may be big enough for Eugenia, but not for Giraffe."

"Better the zoo than the woods west of Missoula," Balleau responded as he scratched his back against one of the hall's great pine pillars. "The wolves over there—not to speak of the rattlers—would make our friend's life very uncomfortable."

"No more uncomfortable, let me tell you," Hal the hippo said, "than he'd find it living among those pistol-packing Survivalists in Oregon."

"True," said Charlton the dragon with a sincere puff of smoke. "I understand they're worse than those my brother defeated in Colorado."

"Yes, Charlton, my friend, they're much worse, let me tell you," Hal agreed. "And they hate hippos."

The entrance of Fergus and Isabella gradually dampened all this noise.

"Take Doomsday Book, Mango," said the queen, "and make sure everyone has arrived. We need a full assembly today. And Rudolph, will you test the p. a. system?"

While Mango flitted about the hall and Rudolph adjusted the microphone, the king and queen mounted the dais that stood beside the royal entrance. As they settled themselves on their thrones and made sure their crowns were on tight, all sounds subsided.

Bo Bo the beaver, who scurried about to pick up bits of straw fallen from the roof and tufts of fur dropped here and there at the last meeting, stuffed this trash in a big wooden basket. Gloria the gorilla took a last luxurious swallow from her flask of banana punch. Casper the crocodile yawned and produced a respectful cough that would have been alarming coming from anyone else. Then silence prevailed.

"Is everyone present, Mango?" the queen asked.

"Yes, your majesty, all present, as you commanded, all except Giraffe."

"Friends, countrymen, citizens of middle Montana, I need not tell you why I called you here today. Each of us, in his own way, has become aware of our dear Giraffe's absence. King Fergus and I have welcomed Charlton and Cauliflower the cooks into our society, as well as Charlton's sister, Mango the maid. We are happy to fulfill the last wish of Giraffe: to allow them to live in his cave—at least for the time being. The king and I hope you will treat both of them and Mango with the same respect we have learned to pay one another. But we understand only too well no one can take Giraffe's place in our land or in our hearts."

"The queen and I summoned you here today," said King Fergus, "to collect and to consider all the signs of our friend we have received one way and another during the weeks—the months—since he has vanished from among us."

"Zane and Zack the zebras," Queen Isabella announced, "have shown the king and me the name tags they shined with a tube of brass polish the foxes delivered to them a few days ago. It was made in Meriden, Connecticut, they told us, but there wasn't a return address on the box it came in. And this very day a package that contained more than a dozen pairs of goggles—extra small—for airplane pilots arrived by FedEx™ from China. One pair, especially made to fit a reindeer, came in the same package. Has anyone else received such another gift, such another sign of our departed friend?"

"I have recently got a little package," said Balleau the bear, "that might have come from Giraffe."

"Tell us about it, Balleau," said King Fergus.

"The last time I saw Giraffe," Balleau responded, "I was wearing my uniform. I had just come from making a very stormy movie, and several of my brass buttons, as Giraffe noticed, had got lost.

"'Dear, dear, Balleau,' he said with a little laugh, 'how shabby you look.'

"The package I received had a card that said, 'To make these shine visit Zane and Zack.' It contained a half-dozen new brass buttons. One had the figure of King Cole; one had a flexing salmon; one depicted Rudolf the red-nosed reindeer; the others projected images of Queen Isabella; and all around each and every one was inscribed, 'The Montana Navy.' I took them over to Zane and Zack, as the card directed, and borrowed a little of their polish."

"That Giraffe," said Rudolph the raccoon.

"Kanga has sewed these shiny buttons in place," Balleau continued. "Behold!"

He waddled a few steps into the crowd to show off his refurbished outfit, made an elegant turn, and then waddled back.

"Anyone else?" asked the king.

After a pause, Felicia the fox spoke up.

"I delivered a box yesterday," she said hesitantly, "to the lions' den."

"The lions' den?" the king responded. "What was it Leo—if you are willing to tell us."

"Water wings, your majesty," piped up Lucy the lion with a giggle, "water wings, 'Extra Large,' in a beautiful pink."

"That Giraffe," said Rudolph the raccoon.

"Water wings?" the queen inquired. "Was there a card, Leo?"

"Yes, your majesty," Leo growled. "There was a card."

"Well, Leo," the queen replied, "what did it say?"

"It said," Lucy piped up again, "'For Leo so you can enjoy those family swimming parties down on The Great Missouri Creek.'"

"That Giraffe," said Rudolph the raccoon.

"Yes, your majesty," Leo admitted with a deep growl. "That's what it said. But if nature had intended for animals to swim, nature would have given us gills—not water wings."

"Gills?" interjected Casper the crocodile, snapping his jaws. "Allison and I swim; we swim for our lives; and we don't have any gills."

"Yes," said Leo with a sarcastic switch of his tail, "but you are reptiles."

"We're not," cried out Billy the beaver, "and we also swim for our lives. That's why all of us, all but Bo Bo, have such fat tails, so we can swim around and build comfortable dams for ourselves."

"I'm a pretty good swimmer myself," bellowed Balleau, "once I take off my uni—"

"Friends, friends," King Fergus broke in, "have we forgotten Giraffe?"

Suddenly, the assembly grew silent again.

Then Queen Isabella rose, walked to the front of the dais, and spoke. "When Queen Isabel and I first recognized Giraffe's departure and I asked her what we would do without him, she said to me, 'The best we can. That's what Giraffe would want.' And the best we can is to live together in peace and friendship, don't you agree? Don't you agree, Leo?"

"Yes, your majesty," the lion responded, shaking his mane. "That is the best. That is what we have all learned from Giraffe."

"And to live together in friendship," the queen continued, "we must practice restraint and tolerance, isn't that so? We must accept one another's differences and honor one another as separate persons. Some of us walk, some crawl, some creep, and some swing from tree to tree; some of us hop and some gallop; some of us swim, some fly, some burrow in the earth; but we are all citizens of Montana, dragons and all."

After a brief pause, King Fergus asked once again, "Has anyone received a further sign of our departed friend?"

There was a long silence, during which Gloria the gorilla offered Dr. Oscar a sip from her flask and, when he refused it, took a savory sip herself. Then when nobody else said anything, Peter o'Possum raised his paw.

"Yes, Peter," said Queen Isabella when her husband had brought the little fellow to her notice. "Have you received a gift from Giraffe—or a sign?"

"I haven't received a gift, your majesty," Peter answered, "but I had a scary dream."

"A dream?" cried the queen. "Do you believe a dream, Fergus, my dear," she asked, "might be relevant to our considerations?"

"It might, darling," he replied. "Let's hear it. We need any clue we can find."

"True, my love," Isabella admitted. "Very well, Peter, let's hear your dream."

"I was walking up the path from my own pine toward Giraffe's cave," Peter began. "I was carrying a big basket of leaves my family had collected: there were tender maple leaves, and oak, and sycamore—they're not easy to find—and sprigs of alder from down by the creek, and new tips of foliage from the elm—"

"That's fine, Peter," King Fergus interrupted. "I'm sure you had gathered a tasty treat for our friend. Now, go on."

"Well," Peter said, taking up the thread, "I had just reached a clearing in the woods about halfway to the cave when I heard a great whirring and, as I listened more closely, a powerful beating of wings above me. I looked up and there in the air, working Charlton's dragon wings with great thunderous strokes, was Giraffe.

"'Giraffe, ' I cried, 'come down, I've got a nice basket of leaves for you. Come down.' But even as I called, he flew higher, circling away from me, higher and higher. As I watched him fly away, I called out, 'Come back, Giraffe, come back.'

"My dear Patsy, sleeping as always beside me, was alarmed by my shouting and woke me up; but I kept calling out, 'Come back, Giraffe, come back, come back.'"

"That's almost the same dream Roo had, isn't it, Roo?" exclaimed Kanga, who couldn't contain herself.

"Maybe you or Roo should describe it," King Fergus suggested as he glanced over at the queen. To forbid Kanga to share Roo's dream would be, not only unkind, but very difficult as well, Fergus recognized. "What was it Roo dreamed?"

"Roo was standing on the airfield, waiting to take off—weren't you, Roo? Not the path to Giraffe's cave, like Peter, but the airfield here beside our hall. But he heard the same whirring sound and then the same beating of Charlton's wings—didn't you, Roo? And when he looked up, he also saw Giraffe soar through the sky and circle round and round over his head. But when Roo cried out and begged Giraffe to come back, Giraffe bent his great neck—didn't he, Roo—and shouted, 'I can't come back. I don't know how these wings work.' Then he vanished.

"Roo was planing to pursue our friend in *The Fly*—weren't you, Roo? But I woke him up before he could take off because I found him crying in his sleep. You were crying as if your heart would break—weren't you, Roo? Queen Isabella, he was crying as if his heart would break."

"Thank you for that dream, Roo," said the king. "It was very sad, wasn't it?"

"Yes," said the queen, interrupting the conversation before Kanga could reply, "but it was a dream after all, Fergus, like Peter's dream. It was only a dream."

"That's true, my love," said Fergus, speaking very mildly because he saw that Isabella was upset. "Yet dreams explain things to us sometimes, don't you agree?"

"They don't explain anything to me," the queen declared.

"Sometimes, I believe," the king replied quietly, "they allow us to tell ourselves things when we're asleep we can't bear to tell ourselves when we're awake."

"Well," the queen said emphatically, "they don't tell me that kind of thing."

"Speaking of dreams," Hal interjected.

"Must we have another dream?" asked the queen.

"No, my dear," the king answered, "if you object."

"Oh, very well," the queen relented. "I don't suppose Hal will be content until he shares his dream with all of us. If it's relevant, Hal."

"I'm afraid it is relevant, your majesty, let me tell you, but you and the king will judge."

"Describe it to us, Hal," said the king. "I'm sure it will interest all of us."

"I didn't see Giraffe in my dream, your majesty," Hal admitted to the queen.

"What use is it then?" she responded. "At this rate, everybody will want to tell us his dream."

"Let's give Hal a chance, my love," said the king. "I don't believe he would take up our time for nothing."

"I was wallowing comfortably in the pond late in the afternoon," Hal began, "when all of a sudden I felt myself sprouting wings, big ones, let me tell you, bigger even than Charlton's and Cauliflower's. I couldn't beat them like Giraffe did, but the evening breeze got caught in them and, before I knew what was happening, it carried me up into the air. 'Oh,' I thought to myself, 'this gives me a chance to search for Giraffe.' And I began to circle over the middle of Montana."

"Did you see Giraffe, Hal, did you see him?" asked Queen Isabella.

"No, your majesty," Hal replied, "but as I soared over the palace I saw your father counting money in the counting house—with your help. The queen, your mother, was eating bread and honey in the parlor, and Marian the maid was swatting at blackbirds in the garden. Then I circled over Friendship Hall. I saw Isabel bandaging the hands of Dr. Oscar the orangutan and Roo landing *The Fly* with Rufus tied to the wing. In the meadow, as I circled further, I could see Ella the elephant stuffing grass and clover into her silo and Zane and Zack sharing some delicious burdock leaves."

"Giraffe gave me that silo," said Ella. "Giraffe and the old king."

"I circled wider through the evening sky until I saw all our friends: Gloria serving Dr. Oscar some banana punch; Kanga serving Peter some mead; Balleau gnawing on fish eyes; Rudolph and Bo Bo pacing off the pavilion; my reptile companions basking together beside Allison's old cypress log; and in the distance the smoke from Billy the beaver's train—all our friends except Giraffe."

"No Giraffe?" asked Isabella, almost in tears.

"No, your majesty, but as I circled back toward the pond, I became aware I was growing a prehensile tongue, as long as, and then longer than, Giraffe's. As I swooped it unfurled like a banner, a great brown and gold banner. It flew out behind me as I soared through the darkening sky. And when I craned my neck—not an easy thing for a hippo to do, let me tell you—I saw the banner was covered with letters."

"Letters?" exclaimed King Fergus. "Did they spell out anything?"

"Yes, Hal," the queen cried, "tell us what they said."

"At first," Hal responded, "as I craned my neck and squinted in the fading light they seemed to say, 'Goodbye, Giraffe.'"

"And then?" asked Fergus, speaking for the whole hall of people who were completely silent.

"When I looked closer," Hal said as if he were actually taking a second look at the banner, "when I looked closer, I saw it really said—"

"What did it say, Hal?" cried Queen Isabella. "Tell us."

"'Goodbye. Giraffe.'"

✠ ✠ ✠

But if Giraffe had wandered away from the middle of Montana, as his friends finally recognized, where had he wandered to?

That was the question Isabella and Fergus shared over their coffee the next morning.

They finished a delicious breakfast of eggs florentine, on which Charlton and Cauliflower had collaborated, and pancakes rockefeller, one of Charlton's specialties.

"Those pancakes were terrible, weren't they, Fergus?" said the queen with a shudder. "What were those great soggy lumps, anyway?"

"Thick slices of banana, dear," said her husband, who was finishing his second helping. "And very tasty they were."

"Great soggy lumps," the queen said again. "But somehow they remind me of Giraffe. We know he's gone now. But where? That question is still unanswered, isn't it, Fergus?"

"Yes, my love."

✠ ✠ ✠

Is it time for a game?

After reading each story, look at the picture again. Do you see a difference between what the writer wrote and the illustrator drew?

There's at least one difference in each picture.

For the answers and other games, go to:

www.GiraffeofMontana.com